Vampire
Solstice
By Starfields

Vampire Solstice

StarFields

First Edition 2006

ISBN 1873483929

**Published By
DragonRising**

Vampire Solstice

First Edition 2006
ISBN: 1 873 483 929

Published by:
DragonRising Publishing
18 Marlow Avenue
Eastbourne BN22 8SJ
United Kingdom
https://www.DragonRising.com

Other fiction titles by this author:

In Serein
Elory's Joy
For You, A Star

Printed and bound by CPI Antony Rowe, Eastbourne

Table Of Contents

PART 1

1: Valia, Essem

The Night Of Blessings

The vibrancy of all this life, of all this youth, quite overwhelms me each time.

Each year that passes, it becomes - more alien, and ever more attractive.

Isn't that strange?

Each year that passes, just a leaf in a breeze, swift they pass, fly away down the endless corridors of time, and they are nothing now - memories, you ask me?

That is such a human thing, such a child's thing.

I don't care for memories.

I let them go; they are not here nor are they now, those who walked then, including all those versions of a me that don't exist at all.

I am here - what more do you need to know?

What of my loves, what of my tears and heartaches, what of my dooms and destitutions, desperations, triumphs, moments of enchantment?

Look.

Leaves gently drifting down into a misty whiteness where all the past sleeps now, far away and quite irrelevant.

Can I travel there?

Of course I could, but what would that accomplish?

Should I get bored of here and now, it might become an option.

I might just follow with the leaves in trailing garments, white the same, just as a virgin bride would walk, her white feet pale and bare, and these old autumn leaves might turn to flower petals as I stride and halt; and there are doors on either side, and every one would lead into a time of past, and I could walk there, live there once again, and see what once I saw, and feel what once I felt - for sure, this is within my power.

I will be honest, and I'll tell you that I won't start on this journey, not until the time is right and time is here for me to step away from all these nows and new adventures; those who are still older than I am, they lie somewhere, and they don't die; they walk amongst their halls of memory and life forever and a day, and they are lost within.

But I, I am of now.

I am of here and so the year has passed again, so swiftly and so beautifully, with silken nights of starblessed beauty, roaring days in deep protection, down inside the earth where all that radiance cannot hurt my fragile eyes, my skin nor set my hair on fire.

It is the night of the furthest drifting.

This night, all of my kind who still walk in the now, we celebrate and mourn alike for this time is so short, and some do hold that it's no time at all, for as the longest night unfolds, it dies the same and will begin to shorten once again as we are ever heading forward on a journey that will never end nor will it ever be the same.

Solstice, they call it.

We call it the Festivals of Blessings.

Here, when we are the furthest from the dissonance the sun produces, we can hear the others all across the worlds, across the voids, most clearly and we sing with them.

All our most holiest of rituals are then conducted; and the elders join us in their far away remembrances, and all and everyone who misses us, as we miss them - it is the night of our remembrance of home and hearth and our night of re-connection, when the wings of night reach out across the endless voids and tell us we are not alone, and we are not forsaken, and that the day will come when we too can rejoin the life that we were meant to live.

All of our holiest rituals are here, tonight; and what could be holier indeed than the audition?

Immortal, And Beloved

This theatre is old.

It is underground.

It is perfectly restored and lovingly maintained; for here, we come together, those amongst the old ones who are willing, to hold the audition - here, we seek for young ones who will leave their lives as men and women and will join us on the great journey.

We are not quite such a secret as the sleepers who know nothing might presume; there are a number who are well aware of our existence.

The governments all know; and all their so called secret branches. Their secret clubs, societies all do know as well, as do all the religions; they keep us for one of those amazing revelations they bestow upon their most ardent of followers upon their various initiations.

They keep their distance, and most wisely so; my kind does not take well to their intrusions for we have our own path and our own unfoldments and we care not for theirs in any way.

Once in a while, you get a madman who will try and lash the sleepers into riot and revolt, who'll try and tell them that there are these others who live blithely right amongst them and who drink the essence of their children to sustain their fragile veil existences; but this never gets much further than a group of medics dragging such a one into a cell, somewhere; a dungeon, somewhere, where they can scream and rant with all the others and no soul will ever listen.

It matters really very little for they cannot hurt us.

No silver bullets, crosses, holy water; all of that is an illusion, just designed to keep the sleeper's fear at bay and give false hope that there might be some form of retribution or of punishment, some way that they could make themselves account for something in their dealings with the likes of us beyond the cattle function of providing food and life.

And a false hope it is.

We are other than, and though we can extend ourselves and reach to them, they cannot reach to us for all the stones, the fires or the bombs they might employ from their material world with their material minds.

Material minds.

Minds of cloth and rag, of wood and concrete, marble minds that do not flow and that is why they cannot touch us, cannot even see us, not unless we make an effort and unveil, enough for them to build illusions then around just who they saw, or what they met.

I remember when this theatre was new.

I remember who ordered the construction; my lover he was, and high amongst the best.

I remember we were young, and laughing at the notion of instead of wandering about to seek for our junior generations amongst the ever burgeoning masses of humanity to have them come to us instead, to kneel and to present themselves, all willing moist, and sensuously there with bodies still so vibrant warm, and beating hearts.

I must remember not too clearly here because you know just what will happen if I do - I will get lost and now is not the time for me.

Let us leave the past and so instead, keep focussed on the now, a long time it has been, and now the theatre does reek of age and great antiquity, and of an ocean, yes, an ocean of young blood that has been shed across the centuries, and the millennia.

Tonight, it is packed with humanity.

It is packed to overflowing - the houses must have been quite active, going out amongst the young ones for recruitment, which is not as hard as it may seem; it is enough for one of us to stand just anywhere and to unveil; and just like water floods most blindly down into a chasm, they will come to us, will hunger for us, will be drawn to us for we are what they always dreamed that they might be.

Immortal, and beloved.

Meruvian

"My Lady Valia," I hear and feel the resonance, I recognise and now a smile begins to slowly spread right from my heart, right from my center, and enters every part of me, transforms my aspects and in turn, I manifest more strongly so that I have eyes to catch his gaze and lips to smile at him.

He is so beautiful.

He always, always takes my breath away.

Ah, what a phrase!

For I don't breathe, and though I have a heart, it doesn't beat - I pulse throughout and interlaced with all that is around me, I draw in strength and purpose always, from all my surroundings, as in exchange, I give my existence to the surroundings in return.

But it is true, when first I lock and link to Meruvian, I stand still for a moment. I stop altogether, in shock at his perfection, and this has been the case since first I saw him, first I tasted him, oh, all these times and times ago.

"Meruvian," I speak his name and colours dance from my lips, they ripple gently but with passion and embrace him, stroke him, set him quite alight the way just I can make him come to life.

He chooses to present in such perfection; but it is a truth about him that he **is** perfection; he is a true prince, an angel born and bred; arisen and now, with his age and his experience, still so much more than once that youngster was I chose from all the other in this very place, at the very first audition, the first we ever held; where first I fell in love in such a way that you might say I've never been the same again.

I can't conceive of him or how he might appear, how he might feel when he has reached an age comparable to mine; for what a king he will become, and what a shining star!

My love and admiration for him is a rapture that is near enough complete; it meets his deep devotion and extraordinary love for me in turn, and where we stand, just where we are, begins to lose cohesion

15

by the power of our contact and the rushing storm we are creating here.

I sigh myself backwards and release this great temptation; and after just a whisper's wind, he does the same and so we stabilise to what we have to be when we are thus together in these later days.

It is quite possible, and I have often thought this as the centuries passed by and not a one like him would cross a path, and thousands did, and none of them could be compared; were not enough to be a shadow or a leaf beneath his feet, that he might be the one.

It has been told and told again that there would be a one who would be born to catalyse the journey; a one of such a strength and passion that he would embrace us all and lift us to the night, to make us one and take us home at last.

Now it is true that in the tales, they don't say that our saviour is a he, and we don't know just how to know the saviour when they come; and it could be just anyone, one of the oldest ones who are so deeply dreaming and so far away already - it could be me.

I've thought this too and many other things just as one does, and yet, to see Meruvian, I can't help it, I can't help myself, I wish he was the one.

I wish he was the one.

The 7th Level

Meruvian and I, his sponsor and his life giver, his first lover and his first teacher, Valia my designation, Essem in rank, are as of yet alone on the 7th floor.

The theatre has seven stands, just like a coliseum; seven layers, seven levels upon which our kind assembles for this wonderful occasion, on this wondrous night of nights; the younger ones are lower down, and there are few who are Essem, who have the right to be right here, on the 7th level and the last before we then ascend to sleep and dream, and will no longer manifest ourselves within this meeting, or upon this plane, quite anywhere.

The theatre is round; and all the floor space will be taken up by the potentials; already, there are many, and when they have all arrived, there will be twelve times a hundred and forty four of them; that many will have been admitted and no doubt a mass of thrice that number will have never gained their entrance here.

The light is soft and subtle; golden and suffused with red; reflecting back from golden decorations, golden wood and the deep russet linings of the curtains and the tiers where our kind is assembling; and as yet, there's only him and me here in the highest stand.

This floor is simply golden red carpet, from the balcony to the walls; and the walls have alcoves with paintings, paintings of our lives and times past; beautiful and all around, a lovely reminder to where we are, and were we are going in a way.

There is no furniture here for we don't need to sit; strictly speaking, we don't stand for we don't have any feet as such, no backs that could get tired and of course, much later on and when the milling dancing crowd of the potentials weaves and moves like seas below, we will fly above them, unseen and unknown, to take our choice, if we should choose to make a choice this night.

Meruvian smiles and sends me his excitement; he feels that this night will be special, that we will have a night to be remembered deeply and I tune and must agree - there is a resonance tonight, a special music in the air, a waiting and whispering that hushes round the empty seventh floor and we are definitely not alone tonight - there are elders here, and that is new, and that is rare, and it makes me tingle through and through and then I spiral sideways as the thought that here might be my own sweet master, finally returned to touch me once again, begins to take a hold, and then unfold within me, and across, around - "Steady me, Meruvian."

The prince of princes is acutely tuned to all my states of being and before I finished my request, he is already there, and places his arms around my waist, draws me to him and into his space of personal protection - warm it is and bright, powerful, deep and wonderful and I draw myself together and I steady here with him.

"Can you feel the elders," I ask of him and he extends himself but though he is so close, he isn't really quite the same as I, each level and each layer has their own manifestations, life; and even though we both are here on level 7, he is young and I am old.

Millennia divide us.

They divide us in experience but more so in development - I can perceive things that he has no eyes to see as yet, no ears to hear as yet, and he still doesn't have the mind and understanding he will need to think about what he has not yet seen, and not yet heard.

Meruvian, my prince, don't worry. One day you'll be a king and you will feel the same as me.

"It will be too late," he tells me. "When that time comes, you will have long left and be nothing but a whispering elder that will spin me out with sorrow and with desperate hope that I might touch you once again - pray there will be a young one of my making then to hold me steady and allay the terrifying grief and loss I had to suffer at your passing."

Time is a curse, indeed.

The sleepers think that we are free of time; that we have conquered time but that is so untrue.

We too are bound by time.

I was not ready to be raising such a one as this Meruvian well until I had ascended high myself; and by that time, and even though he tried, the distance that then lay between us was so vast that he could never close the gap.

And that was just the same with my own master, with my Lord, oh my beloved, oh my Lord, I do not want to now remember what it was when you just went away and you did leave me here, all by myself, with all my hopes destroyed and all of me in ruins, in black ashes and in dissolution, wailing all across the levels and the plains, seeking, searching, knowing that you were not there, knowing that I'd failed to keep in tune with you, and oh! had I tried.

Oh, I tried so hard.

As Meruvian is trying still - is that what drives us on?

Is that the great design and sorrow of our lives, of our existence?

To try and endlessly move forward, try to catch the elder, the progenitor, the one and true and only love?

And then to slow and let your own descendants try the same, try to keep up and get in phase and so it does repeat again and yet again - are we alone?

Will it never end?

We must not think that way.

I must not be that way.

That way is to forsake the time and enter into endless yesterdays - I am not ready, and there's still a chance if I can hold these thoughts at bay that this one here, Meruvian my most beloved prince and saviour, the healer who did bring me life again when I was sure that there could be no more than endless mourning, that this one here might be my king, and we would break for once and always the eternal cycle that has damned our kind in oh so many different ways.

My Lord got tired of the wait, of waiting for me to become his queen and so he simply went away; but I, I shall try and hold it off; I shall try to my last and most intense unfoldment to maintain the here and now; to give Meruvian time, to give him more time than I was given.

That is my pledge; that has been my pledge since first I saw him in this theatre, since first I saw him dance; and knew he was for me, he was perfection, he was beauty, he was there and real and if I could take him, make him mine and make it right, we might arrive together.

This hope has kept me focussed all this time, all these dawns and all these storms; all these mornings, all these nights; it has kept me alive when nothing else could do that for me.

This hope has kept me make a plan to keep me here when all the ones I knew from when I was Arada are long since gone to sleep, so long - so long ago ...

Meruvian speaks into my thoughts.

"My Lady, will you choose this night?"

Oh but I am glad that he is here.

I was right on the verge of there remembering my brothers and my sisters, and all their children, and that's where the trap is that leads you into yesterday and makes it real, and then it does become your prison and you're lost within ...

I will have to keep Meruvian around.

He will have to stay with me from now until I either break or go, or he is ready to step forward and to join me.

My strength is faltering.

I am too old now, too much past, I find it far too hard to keep the balance or to even turn the balance that it tips towards a future. I will need his help.

I often thought that if my master had just asked me to be close to him, my youth would have allowed him to go on beyond what strength he had himself; but it is true, he never asked me, and I didn't know enough, I never, ever thought that he could possibly be gone; I heard these things, about these things, and had encountered howling ones myself but never did I think that this would be my fate, or that it would have been so soon.

I had been away and playing games, enjoying life and all this life does have to offer and it was not until I felt the tearing, screaming pain of his ascendance did I even know this had been underway.

He went to heaven, and I went to hell.

I was still so young, he should not have left me, he must have known what it would do to me, he felt it too and knew it well enough when his own Lady had departed; he told me of it, in whispers and dreams, shadows of dread and horror I did never understand, could never understand until the time arrived and I learned for myself just what it was.

I can't conceive of a more cruel way to be initiated into adulthood.

I can't conceive of a more destructive kind of challenge; and it is little wonder that only few, so very few do make it through and can continue on beyond their master's own ascendance.

Sometimes, entire lines wink out and die; I am quite well aware that there are many in my own descendant line who fell apart when I went mad and simply tore themselves into a million screaming pieces, drifted then away like leaves on a breeze, to be nothing, to be saved in that way, to start afresh - somewhere.

At least for those, the suffering was over; it was a death of sorts, and who would ever think there are so many different kinds?

I step up closer to the balcony and place my gloved hands lightly on the polished wood. As they approach, there is no shadow, no reflection; I notice, smile and make a small but fundamental movement of adjustment to ensure that I should now produce the resonance required to be physical and real enough in all the ways the sleepers tend to judge such matters; should I choose a youngster for my line tonight, they will be much afraid and much in need of gentling and of re-assurance.

Not having a shadow, a reflection or the passing straight through solid objects is quite non-conducive to that end; and further, all it does is fuel more of all the endless questions that the young ones have. Of course they do; they still walk and talk and think the way they do and even though they have received the basic blessing, they have not yet had time to find the way of understanding and of seeing, knowing truth the way we do.

Meruvian has moved to stand beside me and likewise, he makes the resonance adjustment; it is a fascinating, tingling experience to feel him materialise so close to me. It has been quite a while since he and I have been together thus and it is still intoxicating, and I do still enjoy him on this level as I always have. I turn my head to look at him, look up at him; he is tall and stately as a beautiful forest tree, rushing with life but calm and perfectly nourishing.

I sigh with pleasure and relax beneath his shelter, in his shade, in his forest fragrance, forest silence; and I am glad that he appears in darkest green and gold tonight, these are his colours, these are his strengths.

And even so, and even in the resonance that nearly matches physicality, we weave together like a song, I am the wind and he is all the forests, swaying ocean tree tops, finger leaves; and as we weave together, I find myself be drawn more strongly through his roots and youth into the here and now, and we begin to watch the dancers now below, and with his help I see them now, I see them as they are in their own century's attire and not an overlay of many times, of many choosings, as I do these days when I am all alone within the kingdom that is me, a kingdom so wide and so sweeping, so ranging and so all encompassing, that it is getting harder and more difficult with every dawn that passes to remain together or to act upon a single plane, a single point in time, or in a single body.

"My Lady," Meruvian speaks aloud and I shiver like an instrument that has been touched and made to resonate the touch in turn in sound and call, "my Lady, you are far away tonight. Please come and join me here, please come and be here, I desire you to be here, please ..."

As he speaks and pleads with me, I feel a spiral drawing, drawing me down and closer, tighter and inward, and by the time his words have drifted out and far away, I am apparent, I have been evoked and now I'm really here.

I am manifest.

Lady Valia has arrived at the choosing.

2: Steve Burrows, Artist

Grainy Existence

I have never been so terrified, nor so excited in my life.

Always, always I have been alone and felt alone, and always, always I have hoped and prayed, alright, when I was at my lowest I would fall right to my knees and pray to everyone and everything that might be there and listen that there would be, could be, should be something else for me but all of this insanity of nothingness - those people lives, I couldn't take it then, can't take it now, and somehow, deep inside, I always knew that there was an alternative.

There had to be or nothing could make sense.

I read books about secret societies and tried to gain entrance to a few. On the occasions I succeeded, the disappointment burned my skin, burrowed through my liver, tore out my soul.

Ah, it was bad.

The mystery I sought was never there; but still, I could not keep from seeking.

I sought this all my life, and one night, one night I came upon the greatest secret of them all.

At the time, I was living, if you could call it that, in London, and I was working, if you could call it that, as a creative advisor to a bunch of people so stupid that I often thought it would be better to converse with ants, or worms, or perhaps a rock, a grain of sand - alright, so I did converse with sand and ants and sometimes trees, I was insane, I was desperate, I was always falling apart.

I was at an exhibition of what had the nerve to call itself contemporary art, ah well, I guess that's what it is, contemporary stupidity on mass, an excuse for lazy idiots to masturbate their pointless repetitions, raping virgin canvasses and defiling the innocence of a lump of clay.

I don't know why I went that night; I remember thinking that there was no point, that I should stay at home, smoke a joint and make the time just disappear, make the pain just disappear, make it all just go away if only for a moment here and there. I don't know why I got the invitation from the dresser, put on some clothes and made my way through the driving rain that night to the exhibition.

Granular Existence. That was the title. Pointless shit, they might as well have called it and I grabbed some wine and tried as hard as one can try to not see what's in front of you, in acrylics on canvass, huge and somehow the hugeness of the paintings magnified their pointlessness to near implosion point.

That's when I saw him.

That's when I saw Mark Edwards.

He was standing quietly, in an expensive dark suit, with his hands clasped behind his back. He looked anachronistic, 50 years or more out of place, and I just couldn't take my eyes of him.

He was pale, somewhere between 16 and 60, difficult to tell his age, tall, dark hair cut short, reminiscent of an army officer's hair cut. He looked around with a strange air, at first I thought he was nervous or uncomfortable, but then I decided that he was simply dodgy in some way, like he was trying to blend in and not be noticed.

He noticed me staring at him and when he did, he turned his head slightly and looked directly at me, straight into my eyes and my heart skipped a beat.

I remember being very confused by that. It was like falling in love at first sight yet I was not in love at all; I felt discovered, uncovered, undressed - I felt exposed to him and I could feel my head growing hot, my hands sweating around the wine glass and the lights were too bright, too white, too stark and I wished I was ...

Then, he simply turned away and walked away. I couldn't breathe, I wanted to crumble to the floor but I couldn't and then I couldn't stand the idea that he might leave, that I would never see him again, find out more - I must know who that is, I must know this man.

Here is a chance for me to finally learn something new.

I followed him through the maze of exhibits and the studio and then I saw that he entered the toilets at the back and it was an incredible relief, but still I could hardly breathe or speak. I knew the gallery owner and his side kicks, grabbed one of them and made them

24

stand with me until he finally re-appeared, immaculate and so distant, detached, "Who is this? Where has he come from? Who does he belong to?"

The side kick didn't know, said they'd never seen him before, nor had they seen him arrive, and I followed him again and then he got his coat and made for the exit and the panic I felt left me breathless - I ran after him without a thought, ran outside into the rain without stopping to retrieve my jacket, straight out and straight into him.

He was waiting for me outside.

The rain was hard, driving, insanely cold and the wind was freezing; but he, he stood in the rain and he wasn't wet, he wasn't getting wet, the raindrops seemed to go right through him, and I stared at him and couldn't speak, couldn't do anything at all, couldn't think anything but one thing –

"Don't leave me."

For a moment, there it was again - that incredible sensation of him seeing me, seeing into me, stripping me down and out, and then he smiled and reached into his pocket, produced a small business card and held it out to me.

I took it immediately and without thought.

He smiled again, nodded once, then he turned and walked away.

I stared at him simply walking down the street, with other people hurrying by and cars and taxis, bright white lights, red lights shifting, until I could not see him any longer.

The card in my hand was wet with rain splatters, rain rivers and it took some time to focus down enough to read what it said.

It said his name, Mark Edwards, in an elegant if somewhat old fashioned font. And below the name, there was an address. No phone number, no cell phone, no email. Just an address, a London W1 street address.

And that was the beginning of the end. The beginning of the end of this my earthly incarnation.

My joy was such that I could hardly breathe.

Out Of Control

It was over ten days later that I finally found myself outside a perfectly ordinary if expensive and well kept town house. I would have come sooner but I got sick, perhaps it was standing out in the rain that night; either way, I couldn't so much as move for days on end, burning up with fever, drifting in and out of consciousness, and such dreams!

I dreamed of him in so many different ways. I dreamed of him each time I closed my eyes. Frightening dreams. Frightening and exciting both. I didn't know what to do with myself. I didn't think I was gay, I never thought I was, but the way I dreamed about Edwards, I was no longer sure of anything. Days and nights merged into one and my desperation at my state and condition grew all the time - what if I finally got there and he was gone? What if he was waiting, getting impatient, thinking I wasn't interested ...

That I wasn't interested?

In what?

I tried to force myself to eat and drink but it didn't help, it didn't taste right, and I was sick, and always so tired. But finally the spell broke and I could breathe again, think again, well, at least of sorts, and all I could think of was that I had to go there, had to go to that address.

For the first time in ten days I showered. I shaved. I didn't know how to dress, what to wear. He had worn a suit. I had a suit but he had given me the card when I was dressed in jeans - did he want me to be like that? Like he saw me at the exhibition? I stood in front of the bedroom mirror and couldn't believe I was thinking like this, that I was feeling like this, couldn't hold it together, couldn't string my thoughts together, couldn't find a clarity in anything.

I tried, I really tried to think reasonably. He might just be an art collector. He might just be someone who'd seen some of my stuff and wanted me for a commission. I didn't do commissions. I didn't do that anymore. I wasn't whoring myself out any longer. They should come up with their own ideas. But I knew, I just knew that Edwards was no art collector. Perhaps he was a pimp. That thought made me laugh and got me together enough to finally choose a sweat shirt, a pair of jeans, a pair of boots. My usual. No concessions. Take me as I am. I looked in the mirror and knew for a fact that I'd wear a ball gown if he wanted me to. I looked into my own eyes and I was scared shitless. I'd never known anything like this, nothing like this.

I had never even been in love.

Could this be it?

What it feels like?

I called a taxi.

By the time we'd made our way through the thick traffic it was getting dark already again, and I was shaking.

That's not a metaphor.

I was physically shaking.

I saw my hand with the twenty reach forward to the taxi driver and the hand was shaking.

When I got out and into the cold, windy street, the ground was shaking too.

But I was already walking towards the front door before I had decided to do that, and my shaking hand found the doorbell and pressed not once, but three times in rapid succession.

I was completely out of control.

It's Steve . . .

There was a speaker phone at the entrance.

A woman's voice said, "Yes?"

A woman's voice. Not Edwards. His wife? I can't breathe, I can't think.

Out of my mouth comes in a strange voice, "It's Steve. Steve Burrows ..." and I hear it and I think, he doesn't know my name, no-one knows me here, this woman doesn't know me, they're going to tell me to go away, and I really think I'm going to have a heart attack, my head is tight as though there's a steel band pressing inward on my brain, and I still can't breathe properly, and there's a rushing in my ears, I hear something from the speaker but I don't understand it, and then the door clicks and pops open, and I push it open and nearly fall across the threshold.

There is another door in front of me. Like an air lock. Double doors. This second door looks strange, white and with a small panel of stained glass at eye level, it is locked as well. Behind me, the entrance door falls shut with a soft click.

I touch the other door and I can feel that this is metal, with white paint on top. A security door. I look up and see not one, but four cameras, one in each corner of this small entrance space. I knew a guy once who installed security equipment and I can tell that these are state of the art, each one separately mobile and with triple lenses - what is that? Infra red?

A loud sound makes me jump and the white steel inner door has sprung open.

Cautiously, I push it outward. It is dark in the entrance hall.

There is no-one to be seen.

The entrance hall is normal, perhaps a little old fashioned, old fashioned light fittings of the period this house was built, or perhaps retro fittings, hard to tell in this absence of light. Fitted, deep, luxurious carpets.

I hear a movement and look up to the stairs.

On the landing stands Edwards. I know it is him even though all I can see is a silhouette against the stained glass window behind him. I hear his voice.

"Come up, Steve," he says.

A Burden Of Some Kind

I am sitting in a large, old fashioned drawing room on what might be a very expensive antique couch. I am sitting on the edge of the seat, my legs together like a virgin girl, holding my hands together on my knees to stop them from shaking.

Edwards is still standing.

The curtains are three quarter drawn and there are no lights. It is mystical, otherworldly in this room and I am terrified. My head hurts. I feel like crying.

Edwards speaks softly.

"It was good of you to come," he says, slightly hesitantly. I can't place his accent. It is somewhere between public school and American.

"May I call you Steve?"

I finally look up towards him, because I want to feel that feeling again I had at the exhibition, that feeling as though he was connecting to me, reaching into me, actually seeing me, somehow taking something from me, a burden of some kind, something I've long wanted to give to someone, but no-one ever asked.

He comes closer, one step, then two and now I can see his face and I can see his eyes and it is like it was in the dreams, I want to throw myself at him, I want to throw myself at his feet, dissolve to him, just for God's sake, take me, do something ...

He comes closer still and then turns, and sits down in a chair to my right. He leans forward and there is a hungry expression about him, just for a moment, then he puts his head back fractionally and smiles.

"Breathe deeply," he says, and I do, immediately. I take a deep breath and let it out, it comes out like a shuddering sigh.

"Breathing always helps," Edwards says, looks down at his folded hands and continues, "You are an artist, that is correct?"

My mind focuses on the question, and even as it does, I know exactly that he has asked me that to give me something to hold on to, to have that effect on me, that he is controlling me like a hypnotist would, that he is directing my thoughts.

Under normal circumstances, I would have put up one hell of a fight. I won't be controlled, of course I won't, I'm the original rebel without a cause. Rebellion for rebellion's sake, nihilism, annihilation, that's me.

"I was an artist," I reply and my voice is strange, hoarse, far away. I want to ask him outright what he wants from me, why I'm here, but I know full well that I won't be speaking here unless I'm spoken to first. This isn't my show. It is his. He calls the shots. And then I know that this is an audition.

He is auditioning me.

But for what role?

I stare at him, able to do so for a moment as he is still looking down at his own hands. Strong hands, but long, slim. He doesn't lay bricks for a living.

I try to figure out how old Edwards is. I look at his neck, at his hands again. The skin is smooth, silky. Young, very young. But he isn't young. He isn't young, and rain doesn't make him wet.

I finally say it then, it just comes, just comes out, "What are you?"

Edwards becomes still, then he very slowly raises his head and his eyes to meet mine.

"I am a vampire," he says.

Born Again

When Edwards told me that he was a vampire, something strange happened to me.

It was as though a moment of grace fell on me, and in that moment, everything went away.

All the confusion, the fear, the pressure, the uncertainty. All of it just disappeared. And more. All my life's confusion, and there was a whole lot of that, it all started to lift and swirl, and draw away, and then the sadness, and the anger, and the desperation, the fury and the rage, and all I can say is that somehow, all my life up until this one moment just disappeared.

And when it did, I was left in a state of such gratitude and clarity as I never even suspected could exist at all.

I could hear things - so well, so far and wide. Exquisitely attuned, I could hear the cars on all the roads, all around, every different kind, and the buses, trucks and bikes, each one separate, and each one placed with such exactitude. I could hear people, radios, TVs far away, I could hear myself breathing and the windows being touched by the winds outside.

I could see in the dark room, I could see luminescence playing around Edwards' head, around his hands, his neck and shoulders, I could see objects inside drawers and all of that was there, and my own feelings, the steady beating of my heart, the rushing of my breath and every sensation, and all of that was there, all at once, and everything was in its rightful place and combined to create a perfect sense of peace, of reality, of perfection.

As this was happening to me, Edwards was still looking at me and he started to smile, a strange smile of pleasure, joy that was not marred by any form of compassion or even desire. I realised that he must have had such an experience too, and in observing me having this here, he was remembering his own moment of revelation.

I smiled as well then for it was delightful to think that he too had been given this grace, and I was glad he had, very glad indeed for him. What I felt for and with Edwards there was not love, I understood that then, it was completely other than, a kinship that goes way beyond blood and destiny, and I knew that we were the same.

This was a blessing that was mine by rights.

I had been born to this, I had been born for this absolutely, and although it is completely impossible to explain to someone who has not experienced this rebirth for themselves, what you must try and understand is that I never for one moment questioned whether I deserved this, or what or how or why - it was right, and it was finally here, and I was finally saved in all ways.

It didn't matter that he had used the "V" word for it meant nothing.

It was other than.

And although I knew nothing, I knew already that it was what I wanted, what I needed, what was mine by every right.

The Gift

I walked home that night beneath bright stars, and I walked on air.

Edwards had told me that I would have to attend the solstice festival which was a choosing, and that I might or might not be picked to become a one such as himself; he had given me the invitation card, signed with his Lady's name and told me of the location.

As I walked I marvelled at the fact that I was not concerned to not be chosen, after all.

What I had been given this day already exceeded all my expectations for what was possible in this life.

I was perfectly happy to accept my fate now, and whatever this might be; should I not be accepted, I would still always have the starry nights, the sounds and the sensations, the sheer celebration of being alive, and being me, within this fantastic dance of events that surrounds us all but so few of us ever really realise at all.

Nothing could ever hurt me again.

Nothing could ever make me distraught again.

Edwards had healed me of everything, and he had given me everything - the world, the stars, the future and the past, all of it right here and now, and always mine.

I looked up at the stars and I thanked God from the bottom of my heart.

If I was to be a vampire, that would be an honour beyond measure.

If I was not, I would be a man instead.

Either way, I couldn't lose.

3: Mark Anthony Edwards, Cestra Ta Docem

Invitation

I felt myself smiling again as I carefully took my favourite fountain pen and wrote the following words on the invitation card, beneath the print which read:

Adela Bach

Docem

Sincerely Requests Your Presence

For Cocktails

In Honour Of The Potentials For The Festival Of Blessings

On Friday, the sixteenth of December,

At half past eight o'clock

Twentyseven Emery Place, London

Black Tie.

"Dear Steve,

I hope you can make it to this orientation meeting. I look forward to seeing you there,

ME"

The act of writing these words evoked his presence strongly to me; so much so that I could nearly feel him in the room.

I was proud and delighted to have found this one.

He was special.

So special in fact that I can't help thinking he might be the one – my first one, my first transformation. The beginning of my own house.

I shiver most deliciously at the thought and I can feel a power building inside of me, a power and a need both, a wanting and a yearning.

My Lady Adela was quite right.

My time had come.

I was ready to take the next step, become Docem, the master of my own house.

Lovingly, I replaced the cap on the fountain pen and laid it on the table, next to the invitation.

I leaned back in the chair and closed my eyes.

Giving the first release to Steve Burrows had been a most extraordinary experience. I had done this many times before, of course, many, many times since I first arose to my new life as a Cestra, a walker between the worlds, a messenger, a student and a servant both to the young, and to the old.

But this one had been different.

It had been so easy!

Easy, delightful, instantaneous.

He had been so ready, so completely aligned to me, and he had given up his human burdens so willingly and so readily, I've not encountered that before.

It could be that I'm simply better now at doing it.

I smile as I remember the difficulties and struggles that used to surround my early attempts at releasing.

Weeks, sometimes months spent with the candidate; endless talking, endless explaining. Endless emotional outbursts and struggles. Toing and froing. Back and forth before finally, finally they would succumb and give it all up, what remained, bit by bit, time it took and so much attention.

It was hard work back then.

It was nothing compared to the instantaneous flow of release that happened with Burrows. He was lucky to have encountered a Cestra Ta Docem instead of a newly fledged, wide eyed youngster who hadn't seen the light of day in a decade, or two, or three.

Of course, I am immensely fond of all of my conversions and some of them still write to me, once in a while; sometimes I attend their funerals. I love them all most dearly, and no less because they did not go on to be chosen and join the house, or any other. The act of conversion is a wonderful benediction and an amazing gift, either way.

I admire the elders who, in days past so long that it must have been more than a hundred thousand years ago, decided to make it so that every potential will walk away with this extraordinary gift, and never feel that they lost out because they were not chosen in the end to become a member of a house, and a being of our kind.

Gently and with loving precision, I take the invitation and insert it into the thick linen envelope. I take care to address it first to Mr Steve Burrows before I turn it over to seal the envelope with the official seal of the house of Adela Bach.

It will be delivered by hand. A nice little errant for Alexandra, our fledgling Cestra to perform, not too challenging, no direct contact required, a mission that may take place in the dead of night and under gentle distant supervision.

It will be delivered and of course, Mr Steve Burrows will attend the cocktail party. He will look entirely transformed in a tuxedo, possibly the first time he would have ever worn one.

A pre-festival orientation was certainly the first time I had, when I attended a similar gathering, in a house in Westwood, Virginia, over two hundred years ago.

I can't help but smile again and must shake my head. I always associate with my potentials, but this one ...

I put out a strong and clear thought command to Satari, who is my personal assistant at this time and would most likely come with me to assist me in running my own house. She is not one of my own conversions and considerably younger than I am, but we have a good understanding and I know that my Lady Adela chose her for just such a purpose.

Satari appears near instantaneously at the door. I don't have to tell her what to do with the invitation, she knows and will see to it that it will both be delivered, as well as being a most beneficial exercise for our youngster to aid in her unfoldments.

At this time of year, she will need all the stabilisation she can get. We will be attending the Festival of Blessings soon, and that can be an incredibly overwhelming experience which can push a fledgling Cestra back by a decade or more if they're not sufficiently stabilised.

Satari nearly glides towards my desk; she is both dark and fair at the same time, light and slight, but that entirely belies her power and her purpose. I wonder if Burrows will like her too, feel that affinity I have with her in preference as I do, and there we are again.

I've been thinking about this one since first I saw him at the art exhibition. There was really no reason for me to be there, we were so close already to the festival and it wasn't as though we didn't have a good crop of potentials to send to the occasion. We always do.

London is one of those places where they seem to gather quite naturally, from all around the world; there are five houses here, and that's more than you would find anywhere else, and for good reason.

This year, I was as sure as one might be about a future that has not yet come to pass, that the house of Bach would end, and in its place, the house of Edwards would come into being.

My house.

Lady Adela was ready to go.

In truth, she had been ready to go for a decade or so; she was waiting for me.

Ten festivals I had already attended, allowed to share the Docem's level, the only time and place there is an exception to the strict segregation according to age and rank that exists at the festival.

Only those of Docem rank or higher can choose; and I can't be a Docem unless I choose and thus, become a Docem.

A master.

My Lady Adela would hold me and tell me that she loved me and that to wait with me until my time had come was not just an honour to her, but a bittersweet pleasure that was even more poignant because soon enough, it would be over and we would never again be together like we are right here, right now, a Docem and her chosen Cestra mate, completely in love, completely aligned and in a wonderful maturity of experience.

We would never be this close again.

I wonder sometimes if it is this reality that made me hold back at the festivals past, somehow, without me doing it deliberately. But Adela smiled and said that it was all just as it was supposed to be – if there was no-one there who would draw my attention more strongly towards them and thus break my absolute fascination and singular attachment to my own sweet Lady, then it was not to be and none of us were ready to proceed.

I think of Steve Burrows again.

So much sorrow. So much sadness was inside of him, it was near enough overwhelming. It was exploding from him, lit up the room with violent flares of suffering, he stood out like a torch to me and he fascinated me completely.

The stronger a prospective is, the more powerful their emanations are, for the better, or the worse. It is also true that there is a direct relationship between those who would make the best prospectives and their suffering; sometimes it is too much and we are too late to find a most extraordinary candidate and they implode into their own catastrophes and then are lost to everyone.

The thought that I might have missed Burrows is quite painful; I am amazed to notice that it might be even terrifying.

Is he the one?

Will I choose him at the festival?

What will happen if another claims him, one that is far higher in the ranks than I am? I've asked my Lady and she smiled and shook her head.

"It cannot happen, my darling," she said and touched me with such love, with such delight. "We choose by love, we live by love. The one who loves the most will be the one who will succeed in choosing, and there is never any doubt. It doesn't matter if you are Cestra Ta Docem, or Cardor, or even Essem – the greatest affinity, the greatest connection, the greatest love will always win the day."

I feel her absolute conviction and even though I have no grounds upon which I could make a decision either way, I trust her and I go with her decisions, as I always do.

I sigh away my reservations and my nervousness.

Either it will happen, or it won't.

Either I will find someone to love, to choose and to engage, to make my own and thus, to make them like we are, or I will not; next year this time, I will be with my own first love, or with my oldest and my best.

And if I thought of it like that, of course, I was entirely blessed, which ever way unfoldments should succeed.

My Lady Adela

My Lady awaits me.

She is completely Docem, the most evolved stage of the mistress of a house. She has such power that if you close your eyes, you can feel her far and wide, and you want to flow to her like a river, you want to give yourself to her, a wonderful tide of home coming and of absolute blessing in every sense.

She is in complete control over her desires and over her hungers; she is exquisite and as finely tuned as she can be. To engage with her is a rapture, pure and simple; but what makes this rapture even more intoxicating still is the fact that our union can never be entirely completed.

If we were to let the safeguards go and take just one more step, she would instantly devoid me, and absolutely so – I would flow to her and all I am would be a breath of air to her and nothing more, and nothing would be left of me at all.

When we engage, we have to dance and I have my responsibility to withhold myself from her, to give her room so that she can relax and take as well as I control the flow from me to her as best I can.

I am the most evolved stage of Cestra, but I am no match for her, will never be; and so our unions are excruciating, terribly delicious, sometimes starburst wild and yet there is an unknown territory into which we cannot enter, not if we would wish that I should live.

And I don't know how many times I cried and begged her to have mercy, to just let it go, to make an end and take me all and all at once, so we can be together, even if together lasts for just a fraction of a moment, a single splinter made of time, it would be all eternity and finally fulfil my endless need and hers, at that.

I do not know how many times she cried and held me close and showed me once again that this was as it was for our kind; a learning and progression, a test of our strength, of our love indeed for we do have a path, a purpose and a road to travel, each and every one of us, and we must live to do our duty by our kind.

And of course, we do.

But it isn't about duty, in the end.

Unless it could be said that it is the duty of our kind to experience different levels of awareness and of splendour all the while.

I cannot imagine what it will be like to be as Adela is right now.

She is evolving beyond the need for taking life from humans, and from her own kind, or should I say she has evolved beyond that now and only engages in that now for pleasure, hers and ours in equal measure.

She will walk forth from this what was her house without a backward glance and enter her time of Ferata, living alone and wild and becoming of the land, of the sky, the sea, the air and drawing all her sustenance and learning directly from the Universe itself.

She will walk forth and will be gone to me, will be unreachable for centuries perhaps, and when she does return, she will be very different and other than in every way, and not the Lady, not my Docem, not the one who took me in so lovingly and did transform me from a man into an other.

But I shall not grieve, for I am told that I will be entirely occupied with my own loves, with my own Arada and my Cestra, and with the running of my house, with the safety of everyone in my responsibility, and with their evolution.

I find this hard to understand.

I know the theory, of course I do; I have observed and I am faithful that it all should come to pass just as was explained to me and yet, I still cannot conceptualise a state of being where I would be far from Adela and not miss her so much that I would think I'd tear apart.

As I am thinking these thoughts it becomes apparent that at this moment, I would rather be with her than anywhere; soon enough, the time will come when I can never be with her again, not like this, and this time is precious, so precious, and so rare.

So I leave my rooms and make my way to hers.

The house is unusually noisy tonight.

Downstairs, there are the human caterers at work to set up for the party in a few hours. Their voices, their noises and most of all, their emanations spiral through the entire house, fill the corridors and the stairwells with the scent of their youthful, innocent existences. It is like walking through a multi-coloured fog, but now, I think of it in terms of a decoration rather than a distraction as it used to be when first I re-emerged to face all that again, from this new vantage point as was.

Adela knows that I am coming, and she knows why I am coming.

I do not pause before her door but make the effort and de-stabilise, precisely and just enough to pass through the door without having to open it.

Adela sits in her bedroom, at the far end by the heavily curtained bay window, in front of a great mirror, clad only in a clinging garment of pure and subtle silk. Her eyes are in the mirror, and she is reflected perfectly and looks at me through the mirror; I smile and manifest a little more tightly, and so my reflection then arises behind her as though I stepped out from a morning mist.

Adela is incredible.

She is simply the most beautiful woman I have ever seen, tall, strong and subtle; as fair as a glacier at dawn with her clear blue eyes and white blond hair that falls in natural waves across her bare shoulders, cascades down her back, light and electric, a mermaid under waters of an ocean that is cold and so pure, so eternal, bright white and blue, dancing with life and ancient awareness.

I close my eyes and melt into her presence as she accepts mine with equal admiration. She enfolds me, she empowers me and it is true that I have never known to be of worth or value until Adela showed me what she saw and tasted when she touched my heart, my soul.

I place my hands on her fair shoulders, my mouth into her hair and breathe her in, drink her in, her state of being that holds an amusement on this night, a tingling expectation that lies like an emerald strand alongside the rivers of her usual existence.

Beneath my hands, my mouth she is turning, and I turn with her, so we kiss; she takes my breath and I take hers and so we both pass knowing of each other to each other and combine, and there is the temptation, the urge to take it on, to take it further, to connect more deeply and more deeply still, one circuit after the next, one exchange flowing after the other, until it is a rushing storm, becomes a tumbling cascade that takes on a life of its own, a desire and power for fulfilment that is beyond the scope of words to understand.

Regretfully, oh! Always regretfully we call a halt and disengage enough so that we might be conscious once again of our surroundings and on this night, Adela choose to address me through her voice, in words that resonate with layers, levels, meanings and instructions up and down and far and wide.

"How long is it to go?" she asks, and that is not a question for she knows exactly just how long an interval remains before we both will royally descend the stairs and take our places in the drawing room, and watch with mounting joy and much amusement as the potentials slide into the room, half aware and full of life, and full of questions.

What she is doing is to ascertain that I am in the flow, and if I need her help to both be present and aware, with all things ready and arranged, so that the evening will be wide open and a good event for all who gather on this night.

There was a time when that would not have been required; we were stable and completely functioned in our roles and places, a dream team she had called us and we worked together in that way for more than a century, before the changes started to unbalance what had been the perfect situation and she moved ever more towards her next unfoldment as Ferata, and I as Docem.

Still, Adela feels entirely responsible for me. In some ways, I know that she remembers me as that – not as a dreaming Arada, not as a fledgling Cestra, not as her chosen mate but just as these potentials we will see tonight, a new and frightened being that is so vulnerable, so excited and so absolutely in her power.

Love at first sight.

It is true, and I am intrigued by the fact that this has never changed. I only know first hand how the unfoldments change you, and still it is the first moment, the first meeting that is the clearest and brightest of all the memories, the first time you saw a one, the first time you felt that resonance, that drive to union and to absolute submission.

I share this with her and she laughs, turns away from me, picks up a brush and begins to stroke her bright hair. It shines and sparkles in the gentle light provided by two candles inside a crystal shade that sits to the right of her on the dressing table, the only illumination in this room.

Adela says, "I can't wait to see your Mr Burrows. You certainly are most impressed."

I smile from behind her and she takes my smile into her shoulders, lets it flow between her shoulder blades and down her spine, down her back.

"I keep thinking about him," I say. I know she knows, for when I think about him, she will think about him too, thus is our connection. A thought occurs to me.

"What would happen if you were to choose again, at this festival?"

The brush stops in mid sweep and Adela looks up into the mirror, finds my eyes.

"Then, I will stay a while longer."

It is strange how that possibility had never occurred to me before.

Of course. If Adela should find a one to make a union, she could not move on and leave them, new, naked and vulnerable. She would have to stay and see them through to Cestra – and that would change everything.

My heart beats faster as I consider the possibility of what it would be like if both of us were Docem, the leaders of separate houses and we would come together ...

"You know that is not allowed," she says softly, regretfully and I think this was the first time that I had felt from her a direct and absolute resistance to the Covenant, the eternal laws that govern our kind.

The Covenant

In the times when I was Arada, the not-yet-born, drifting in white silence and in never ending comfort, I learned many things.

I learned these things not in words, and often not even in visions or in sounds, but they were knowings that became a part of me as my Lady and her Cestra drank my humanity away, a little bit at a time, and replaced my structure from the inside out with their own.

I remember a story, very clearly and in preference to many other things I learned and I was taught, knowings and inscriptions, some of which felt so old, so very, very old ...

I remember a story of two Docem who met and fell in love, and entered into a union from which neither could escape and which destroyed them both, and all their line, their houses and all their dependents.

A union between two equals is impossible.

Neither can safeguard the other; neither can resist the other; and as each begins to feed upon the other, the circuit becomes faster and faster, rushing ever more out of control until it tears them both to pieces.

It was one of the very first things that I learned, and truly understood because I knew just how it was, what it was that happened when your Docem starts to feed from you and takes your life force from you, and what is most astonishing about the process is that you would give it up so willingly, and more, that you would rush forward, throw yourself in wild abandon at your Docem, even at a Cestra, for it feels so good to be relieved of that, it feels so right and just as though it was what you'd been waiting for all your life.

I don't know just why that should be so; but I will learn in my own time, when as Cardor I will help to shape and to police the Covenant. I will learn everything there is to know about our kind, and our purposes, our path. Instead of knowing certain things and wondering just how I know, I will experience clarity.

This time will come; it isn't here and there's no need for me to wonder or to worry; for now, all I have to concern myself with is to follow the Covenant, and to enjoy my existence in every way and whatever stage or challenge might be with me at the time.

The Covenant protects us, it guides us, and it gives us a way to handle the enormous time spans that are part of our unfoldments.

The first law of the Covenant is that we are ruled by love.

When I became aware of this, the basic law of the Covenant, I knew it to be true at once. I knew this in a very different way from how a human might perceive this statement; for our kind does not consider love to be a concept, an idea or just a word.

To us, it is reality.

Reality of such power and such force that we both live and die beneath its cruel and glorious wings.

Only those who are loved are chosen to be amongst us; only those amongst us who can love will choose. We fall in love with power and with a passion that is unknown, unheard of amongst humans but for rare and distant tales and incidents which are repeated for the youngsters through story, song and tale.

It is this love which guides our conduct, binds us, holds us tight and it prevents us from transgressions even if we wanted to commit them.

My Lady Adela cannot hurt me. She cannot kill me, not even by accident; she cannot choose to kill me, hurt me or destroy me for she loves me far too well and my well being is beyond her own.

And so it is for me as in return, I love her just the same – she is my alpha, my omega, the rising sun and all the heavens and there is no higher power that could sway me from my course to help her, to protect her in all ways and yes, including from myself as well.

Adela made me. She chose me from more than a hundred thousand, for she had not chosen in a hundred years when first she saw me at my festival. She chose me as I chose her and our bond of love is thus unique amongst our kind.

Yet everyone within her house and everyone who is connected as we all are through our unions and exchanges is in love as well, as there would never be a one amongst us who was not conceived in love to start with, raised and reared in love and with the time that passes, the bonds are ever strengthening, ever deepening – none of us can transgress against another, no matter what the rank, and we all serve each other, one and all.

The second law of Covenant is that of evolution.

No thing should ever get between a one and their unfoldments; unfoldments are what make the Universe remain alive and to transgress against unfoldments is a death, a deadly sin indeed.

We are exquisitely aware of the unfoldments, and even though they move so gently that it may appear that nothing changes for eternity, this isn't so; we have our time, but it is different from what we once knew when we were human still.

Our time spans are far greater yet and at the same time, they are infinitely more precious as each moment, every second is a step upon the path from here to there – we are growing, learning, and unfolding all the time.

I often think how blessed we all are that these two laws in action do create a situation where not only there is love, but it is new love all the time – as I change, as I grow, so does my Lady and each time we come together, each of us is new and there, we fall in love afresh, bright new and so exciting!

It is as well that first when we are new and young, we sleep and dream for many years, for our skill to move from one excitement, from one joy into the next without a backward glance or wanting to repeat a something that has gone and is now of the old is something we all have to learn, a human life entrainment that must be dissolved and absolutely laid aside or else we waste our wonderful eternities.

My own unfoldment is my highest duty; but also bound by love and service, it is my responsibility to assist in the unfoldment of the others that I love, and all others of my kind in every way I can.

I understand the Covenant; it is alive, it is within me and all around me. It is who I am and what greater joy or pleasure could there be?

And yet, my Lady spoke in true regret when the idea of the union of two equals came to me – the Covenant forbids this, but here is the question.

This law is not the first.

The first law of the Covenant is love.

I understand, and I shiver.

Love overrides all.

If our love was to dictate it, we could enter into the union of two equals.

And we would not have broken any law.

In the mirror, my Lady Adela smiles at me.

She initiated this train of thought and catalysed my understanding to perfection.

"Ah, my Lady ..." I sigh and go to her, kneel before her and place my head into her silky lap.

She strokes my hair with smiling fingertips, and so we are when from below, a bell is heard to ring and now I smile as well for we have truly lost ourselves in time tonight.

The first of the potentials has arrived.

Focus On Adela

My only personal conversion this year is Burrows. Our house is small, Adela has been keeping it to the minimum in preparation for her departure and to make it easier on everyone to find new arrangements. We only have seven Arada in the Underworld, and apart from me, there are only two other Cestra – and none of these are Adela's own, they are all fosterlings now.

Satari and Alexandra have found five potentials, so we are expecting six guests tonight – six bright new humans, grateful humans, confused humans.

When I was young, the house was much bigger still and there would be dozens of these; it was a big occasion back then, very lively, so much energy all around.

Tonight, everything is rather muted.

There is a silent expectation of the end of the house that has been getting ever denser these past few years, and with that comes a sense of sorrow of the passing of what had been a wonderful time in our unfoldments, coupled with the not knowing what would happen next.

My Lady and I take our time to get ready, and when we are we get involved with one another, lightful and delightful playing to pass the time until Satari brushes us with the invitation to descend and meet the new potentials.

I smile and through me, Adela too becomes intrigued and then excited. I hope she will see what I did see when I invited Burrows; I hope she will find him a good choice and I hope my judgement has been sound.

Outside Adela's rooms, Satari is awaiting us. She leads the way down the stairs and we remain in the hallway, outside the formal reception room, until we have been fully announced with name and rank, and then we step inside.

The reception room is splendid; softly yet radiantly lit with many candles in crystal chandeliers. At the top end, two elderly human caterers are standing quietly with serviettes across their arms before the buffet table. Alexandra is sitting in one of the corner sofas, looking amused and extremely haughty with two adoring male potentials, and the other four potentials are clustered together in a tight and frightened group by the great fire place, each one clasping a crystal glass of champagne and staring straight at both of us, then their eyes slide off me and focus completely on Adela.

I side step my focus and attune more to their state of being, and I don't have to try very hard to remember just how amazing it is when first you meet your first real Docem.

With the Cestra, there is a sense of comfort there – well, they are a lot like us, the potentials would be thinking, this isn't such a change, not such a big deal. But when they see their first real Docem, they begin to understand that they are dealing with something they have never known before at all.

Every one of them can feel Adela into the marrow of their bones.

Every one of them can hear her thoughts, and every one can see the radiance that surrounds her, beautiful veils of drifting colours, silken, pastel, winds of change and of pure beauty, of pure power.

With Adela, and especially on this night, there is still more to make it even more memorable an occasion for these humans – she is already part Ferata, and there are forests in her trail, soaring mountains in her wake and starlit nights, whispers of mysterious strangeness and universal knowing, wide flung wings of day and night in everlasting harmony.

I shift my focus to find Steve Burrows, who said he was an artist in the past tense, and I must smile.

He looks quite the part in his brand new tuxedo, and he has already moved a little into an acceptance of that form of attire, into a compromise; Alexandra's two young men by comparison are still very much humans who are chafing uncomfortably in their hired evening wear.

Burrows is older than is usual or average for a potential. Most are found on or around my age, sometimes a little younger even, but he is already marked by time, by suffering. There are sharp lines in his face, around his mouth and around his eyes but they give him character and do not detract from a basic grace and inner strength that holds him upright and tense, even when he tries to appear relaxed in gesture and in stance. He must have been battling whether or not to get a hair cut; I'm glad he decided not to because his long, fine, untidy blond hair gives him a real artist's flair and in this light, a halo, too.

Burrows is staring at Adela, his mouth is half open and like all the others, he is completely under her spell, completely entranced.

And then he shocks me absolutely by slowly closing his lids and when he opens them again, he is looking directly at me.

Not only is he looking at me, he is attempting a move towards a union!

I am shocked again and my shock transmits to my Lady who turns towards me and the entire room takes a breath, unravels, startles aware and awake and for a moment, no-one knows just what to do exactly.

I can sense Adela's amusement, tinged with a little note of wonder and then she says, "Mark, Satari, Alexandra – please introduce me to our young guests."

I look to Burrows and nod to him, and he comes forward, hesitantly, clasping the champagne flute in both his nervous hands.

I smile at him encouragingly before I step aside and say, "Mr Steve Burrows, this is Lady Adela Bach, the Docem of this house. My Lady, this is Steve Burrows."

Adela's amusement deepens as she holds out a gloved hand to him, palm down.

Burrows takes it with utmost caution and I know for a fact that even in the presence of this extreme Docem, he has just debated with himself if he should shake her hand and refuse the kiss. I have to take a moment to contain myself, and Adela's amusement is such now that it is hard to keep composure.

Burrows leans over my Lady's hand and performs a bow over it, doesn't dare to touch it with his lips, and when he straightens he has blushed deeply.

I tune to her more tightly and I am relieved to note that he does not only amuse her, but that she has a sense of fondness for him, feels a kindness for him and so she does not say anything else, just smiles gently and then moves on, between us, leaving her fragrance in her wake as she flows across the room towards the fire place, where Satari will make her introductions next.

"Tell me to keep breathing," Burrows says to me and then blows out a long breath through pursed lips. I smile and go to stand beside him.

The next potential, an otherwise quite plain girl with tight, long brown curls kneels and nearly falls at Adela's feet.

"Wow," Burrows says. "So that's what a vampire master – mistress ..." and there, words fail him. He was going to say, "looks like" but then refrained from using that description; feels like, appears like, makes me feel like?

That and so much more.

I wonder what he would paint, if he would try to paint her, the first time he saw her, just beyond the doorway here in this room, tonight.

"Would you like to sit down for a while?" I ask him and he startles out of his reverence, his fascination and nods immediately.

"Yes, please," he says. I lead him to one of the sofas that arranged in groups for privacy and intimacy, in the corner by the buffet so he can keep viewing the entire room and everything that happens here from a safe vantage.

As we sit, one of the waiters offers me a tray with champagne. I take a glass, nod my thanks and become aware that Burrows is watching me now, with an intent and hungry expression. He's going to ask me if I'm going to drink this. If I drink, and eat, or if it is all blood ...

"Do you still eat? And drink?" Burrows asks.

I smile and answer in action, by first scenting and experiencing the wonderful tiny sensations of the champagne against my lips, under my nose. Then I close my eyes and take a long, slow drink, tracking all the small explosions of taste and texture all the way, and the energies as they disperse and intermingle with my own.

I like champagne. It is a miniature festival, every sip, every glass.

Across the room, Alexandra and her two potentials are getting ready to meet Lady Adela. I lay back and watch Burrows watching them, watching their reactions to Adela and how it reveals so much about them, both who they are and who they're trying to be, two very different affairs of state, indeed.

Alexandra's boys are very good looking. One is white, the other of colour; they are both strong, well grown and congruent. Eager to please, intelligent undoubtedly; young princes and I'm sure if they were to join us here and become Arada, I would grow fond of them in time, but as far as I am concerned they lack that special something that attracted me to Burrows.

"How have you been," I enquire easily and he turns around to me. This time, our eye contact is brief, a flash, before we both withdraw and look somewhere else. This is a mutual decision, and that in and of itself is remarkable. I am Cestra Ta Docem, and he is only a potential. He has power, this one.

"It's been amazing," he answers me, returns to watch Adela with Alexandra and her boys but continues to speak. "It's like I've woken up from a long, long sleep. A nightmare that used to be my life." He pauses, puts his glass on the polished table before us, next to one of the many crystal coasters, then turns right in the seat and straightens, requests full eye contact. I steady myself and look into his eyes, and he says, "I don't know what's going to happen, but whatever it is, I wanted to make sure to thank you. Thank you."

I don't know what to say to that. He is, if he knows this or not, a still, ancient stream, deep underground, full of clarity and strength. When he digs that deep, he will discover this about himself.

"It was a privilege," I respond and then we both nod at the same time, sigh at the same time, lean back in our seats at the same time.

Adela is through with Alexandra's boys. She moves into the center of the room, which causes everyone to focus on her exclusively once more, and says gently, "Your Cestra will answer any questions you might have about the festival, or the choosing. Please enjoy the stay in my house." She smiles, turns and makes towards the exit; Satari rushes to open the door for her, and to close it behind her once she has left the room.

I feel Burrow's disappointment at her leaving, as well as his inordinate relief at her leaving, which is reflected and amplified by all the potentials as though it was my own.

Now, we could get down to the purpose of this night.

Riversmooth

I don't get out much these days.

To find potentials, amongst other errands, is a practice task for the young Cestra; to convert them is an essential training exercise that stabilises them in their new states of being, challenges them and teaches them about their personal otherness in comparison.

Like so many other things we do, the choosing and conversion of potentials is an exquisitely multi-layered thing with many meanings, many, many different strands of purpose.

The third law of the Covenant is that of the preciousness.

It means that truly, between us there is no hierarchy, no rank of any kind. The potentials don't understand this, they always misjudge the idea of there being unfoldments from one state to another as being a linear progression towards power and yet more power.

Of course, the older we become, the more we know and understand; of course, we become more powerful with the passing unfoldments in many senses.

However, it is the youngest Cestra who indeed decide who ever will become a Taray one day, for they pick the potentials, and they alone.

It is an incredible responsibility and I well remember just how astonished I was when I did move amongst the humans in their world and try and seek a one who would give me a resonance, an indication that they might be in potential one of us.

It has been a long, long time since I discovered someone and I did not expect to be doing so again.

For a hundred years or more, at this point of the evening, I would be with Adela, and we would exchange amusements and insights about the new crop of potentials, and about the young Cestra, and how they arrived at their specific candidates.

To be here with Burrows is like a time warp, or more precisely, a state warp.

I am not a little uncomfortable about all of this. I really should not have become involved with a potential at this late stage; this might account for the pure speed of the conversion when it should have taken a gentle time of learning, of exchange of information, many meetings, a slow building of trust and recognition, questions asked and answered, and most importantly, time for the potential to reflect on what it was they were about to enter here.

Burrows has missed out on all of that, and more to the point, there is no time left now to explain it all. He would have to decide on intuition – and what would happen should he come to regret his decision? Is this possible?

As my discomfort grows, Burrows becomes more nervous and uncertain.

He can see that Satari and Alexandra are light and at ease with their potentials, drinking and talking, movements in harmony and familiarity.

I can see that my Cestra sisters are very skillfully engaging in polishing their people, aligning and removing any left over disturbances, to make them more attractive still, a last minute intervention right here in their own house, with their own Docem lending insight, wisdom, strength and support at the other levels, so that the potentials should be as attractive as possible and represent the house of Adela Bach with dignity, and splendour.

I, on the other hand, sit in the far corner with my strange potential and I second guess myself, spiral about inside myself and question whether he should even be here.

This will never do.

That night, I made the decision to go outside. I wandered around and entered the exhibition. I had a sense that I should be there, and when I saw Burrows, I couldn't help myself, I had to pick him. I didn't even think about it much at the time. Adela was very surprised when I related the incident to her on my return but accepted the entire situation immediately as an unfoldment. I often wonder if I will ever flow as freely as she does, swim in time so elegantly, forward she moves so easily and not like I, who seems to spiral back and back and back again before I gain any distance at all.

I force myself to steady down and to become clear, clean and flowing, inside and out.

Riversmooth.

The first and simplest of all Cestra invocations. I am supposed to be Ta Docem and I really need this child's device to keep my balance on this night.

As I begin to ripple and to flow into the perfect state alignment beneath a shield of flowing silver water, a sense of peace and safety begins to enter the entire room just the same, begins to spread across the house and everyone responds – I can feel Adela sigh with pleasure in her rooms above, Satari and Alexandra relaxing, even the two old human waitors who have been in this house on many previous occasions shift down and stand more comfortably.

The only one who seems completely untouched by riversmooth is Burrows. Actually, no, he isn't untouched. He is responding badly. He frowns and leans further away from me, holds his champagne glass close to his chest and shakes his head.

"What the hell are you doing?"

I can hear his thought as loud and clear as though he had shouted it into the room. It causes a ripple in my riversmooth, but only for a second.

In the spoken word, I respond.

"We are here tonight so that you may put questions to me, and I will answer them."

Burrows sighs but does not relax. He shakes his head again. He doesn't know where to start. He plays for time, takes a drink from his glass, then another. Finally, he asks, hesitantly, "Does it hurt?"

Even in riversmooth, I am amused.

"No. Not at all."

Burrows reflects on this and tries another drink from his glass, but his glass is empty. He places it on the table, again to the side of the coaster with absolute deliberation. I find that fascinating. It is a small protest, but a noticeable one and one which he has chosen to make.

As I am not saying anything, he sighs, sits back in the chair and looks at me. He has beautiful eyes, bright eyes, challenging eyes. In riversmooth, he cannot touch me or reach me from outside and I can see the bereavement this causes him, the disappointment, then, the anger.

That is an old anger and it has survived the conversion, which is quite remarkable.

"So," he says quite pointedly, "Tell me about the blood drinking, the people killing, and that whole immortality lark. If that's why we're here. Give me the low down, Mr Edwards. The managerial version." He crosses his arms and then his legs as well and looks across to me a challenge.

I answer simply. "We do not drink blood. We transform people into our own. We are immortal."

Burrows draws a breath in through flared nostrils as he receives this information.

"No blood?" he asks, cautiously.

"No blood. I believe it is a metaphor for the flow of life inside a person, inside anything and everything."

"So you people are – energy vampires?"

I shrug. "As good a description as any. But essentially correct."

"How is this transformation achieved?"

"Over a period of time, we take the existing flows and slowly replace them with our own kind. When this replacement process is complete, so is the transformation."

"Over a period of time? How long?" he asks, curious, and his rigid posture of rejection begins to soften.

"It depends on the individual and the house involved and it varies. It can be as short as ten years and sometimes, it takes centuries."

Burrow gasps and his eyes are wide in shock. "Centuries?" he says, helplessly.

"Centuries," I respond lovingly and I can feel my state of riversmooth beginning to dissolve, shift and shape into another state, that of remembering the wonderful peace, luscious drifting, deep restoration that is the blessing of Arada.

"Come with me," I say and rise. "Come with me and meet our beautiful Arada."

Mirror Transformation

At the end of the corridor behind the staircase, there is a great mirror. It is clearly very old, but at the same time, it is immensely clear, brilliantly clear. It reaches from the top of the picture rail right down to the skirting board and is bordered by a thick frame of exquisite carvings inlaid in fresh, bright, shining gold.

As we approach the mirror, Burrows sees that he alone reflects even though we are shoulder to shoulder, and he keeps looking at me and then back at the mirror which still shows only him, then he stops me, about ten feet away from the massive mirror.

Hesitantly, he reaches out and touches my upper arm, lightly, then more insistent.

"You – feel so real," he says and shakes his head, looking back and forth between the mirror and me in the corridor.

"I am real," I say, "I am right here. I am manifest, but there are many different levels of manifestation. Watch the mirror."

He looks into the mirror and I gently manifest more tightly; the mirror trick is a fine tuning that all young Cestra have a great time practicing with much giggling upon their first emergence. As I manifest, there appears a shadow at first; an undefined swirling that takes on more and more shape and form until the mirror reflects perfectly two men in black tie evening dress, one dark haired, one fair; one composed, and the other amazed, appalled and delighted in equal measure.

"Wow," he says. "I get to learn to do that?"

I find his eyes in the mirror and tell him very seriously, "There are many more potentials than will be chosen. There is a high likelihood that you will not be chosen at the festival, statistically speaking. It is only a possibility, a potential, that is all."

Burrows nods and sighs. "I understand," he says, "But ..." and then he bites his lip and strangles the rest of the sentence.

I turn towards him and look at him directly. "Speak honestly," I tell him. "We have not much time. The festival is only five days away."

Burrows gives a small submissive nod. I gave him a direct command and he will have to obey it, then try and work out why he did at another time.

He says, "I am thinking that you have already chosen me, and that I am not just any potential."

Gently and quietly I say, "All potentials feel that way."

Emotions pass in ripples across his face, his stance and bearing and there is an enormous sadness that sweeps up inside of him, crests across and falls on me in an instance; I am enveloped by it and it is such a strange sensation, such an old, old occurrence that has come back from the dungeons of the past to punish me for having been so unkind as to say what I did in the way I said it.

Speak honestly. There is not much time. The festival is only five days away.

I turn to face him squarely. "I am sorry," I say. "I shouldn't have said that. And it isn't true. You are right. You are not just any potential. It is – extremely unusual, let me say – for someone like me to – recruit. And you are right in saying that I have already chosen you."

I was surprised at how difficult I found it to tell this human about my motivations. With another of my kind it isn't necessary to explain yourself, your motives, your doubts and your insecurities; they already know them intimately. We are of the house, we are family, we know everything about each other and the only thing that remains an everlasting mystery is the unfoldments yet to come. We are a single system in truth and if I don't know something about myself, the others will and through them, I will know it too.

But here I realise that I did indeed go far beyond a simple potential recruitment; that what happened between Burrows and I in the street outside that gallery was a true breach of conduct, probably even a breach of the Covenant. This thought appals me so much that not only do I wink out from the mirror in an instant, but that Adela did instantly manifest in the corridor behind us, entirely alarmed at the sudden disturbance in my states of being, to which she is linked as though I was part of her own body.

"Beloved," she says and resonates it across the levels and the layers, deep and wide and then there is only she, and she is strength and beauty absolute, safety and radiance all at once, movement re-established, flow regained.

"What have I done?" I ask of her in helplessness, and Adela is surrounding and soothing. "You are engaging an unfoldment," she tells me, "Beloved, remember the Covenant. Remember the Covenant."

The first law. The first law is love. All else is secondary, subordinate, immaterial.

"Are you telling me it is allowed to choose outside the festival?" I can't believe where my understanding of the Covenant is taking me.

Adela is very still, very real and very serious. "It is only allowed if it should happen," she replies with care. "Under any other circumstance, it is indeed, a serious breach of the Covenant."

I am completely caught off guard. I thought I understood the Covenant, that I had learned a law that was both just and beautiful, a law that doesn't exist to punish but only to protect and foster our development, a law that is there to guide us, allow us to be free of pain and fear inside its eternal halls.

But here, in this corridor, so ethereal that Burrows can no longer see us at all and hardly senses our presence, I begin to catch a glimpse of the true strength and unbelievable age of the Covenant, how it is not this one thing that I thought it to be at all, but instead, an organic structure that is as changeable as we are ourselves, and as evolving, all the same.

The Covenant itself is love. It is unfoldment, and oh! so very precious!

As I begin to sense, and see, and understand, I also feel a different strength, a different level now begins to rise in me, this is the essence of the Covenant and it is causing an unfoldment, a transformation as I engage with it and through it, gain an entirely different understanding of its purposes, and even of its relationship with all my kind.

I am speechless, helpless in this newness, in this ancient brilliance and in this state of pure amazement, of humility.

My Lady Adela is behind me and beside me, either side of me, fountain columns of pure strength and of support, and as I change and I transform throughout my matrix, through my structures and my times, as I am Docem, newly born, we both then also know that it was true, that we had silently and deep inside created in our unions a treaty which decreed that we should stay together, ward off our subtle new unfoldments and remain, just where we were, but that in truth I have ascended – I am Docem and she is Ferrata.

Our transformation has occurred.

4: Alexandra Anna Maria Zyskowska, Cestra

Pain And Confusion

There was something strange about this year's festival. We all knew that, we all felt it, in our different ways. I am young and I don't know so much, but I have been to over twenty festivals before this coming one, and have more than two dozen potentials to my name.

Of course, we were all waiting.

We were waiting for Lady Adela to leave us, and for Mark to take his place as the chosen Docem of the house.

Sometimes, Satari and I would engage and share our thoughts about that.

This was a lonely house, an old house on the verge of becoming extinct; and sometimes, we would wonder what it might be like to have been brought into a house in its full glory, where a fully focused Docem, straight inside their own unfoldments, would be leading dozens of Cestra, with more than a hundred Arada to care for, and an air of summer nights and coloured lights, of festivals and dancing in the air.

Don't get me wrong, I am devoted to the Lady Adela in all ways, but it cannot be denied that I wish that my own dear Lord, the one who choose me and transformed me, would have been here with me, for me, engaged with me, sharing the unions like the Lady Adela shared her time in preference with Mark.

He was her own and her own choosing; their bond was exquisite and so deep, so other than what I knew from my own Lord, and that was just the same for my dearest of all sisters, Satari.

We had been both delivered here, straight after our unions, the first, the deepest and the best of all the unions there could be, and we had been Arada here, and felt the deep and unassailable caring and love from our Lady Adela, but just sometimes, just sometimes, I wish it had been different.

Tonight is such a night.

Tonight, as everything recedes around us and we are swept up and right away into the strangest of unfoldments, tonight, as I am clinging to Satari as she is clinging tight to me so that we won't be lost in the unknowable exchanges, shifts and resonances that surround us, that buffet us like powerful winds, that throw messages at us we cannot decipher and that invade our matrix, causing us a chaos of unknowable confusion, yes, and pain, I cry for my own Lord, I cry to him for help although I know that to do this constitutes a serious breach of the Covenant.

There is no response that I can perceive; and the confusion becomes greater still as Satari too begins to cry, and now the Arada are swept up as well into this madness and their dreams become uncomfortable, disturbed; the Arada are innocents, they are children, and they should not be suffering like this!

I cry to Lady Adela to make it stop, to end this what should never have been known to us, Satari joins the cry and so do those of the Arada who already know enough but our Lady does not hear us, does not feel us, she is gone and we are now without a Docem, there is no protector, there is no-one at all who will come to my rescue, and this causes a renewed and powerful onslaught of disturbance that has me cry out in pain in every way I can, I cannot stop myself although I know that I am making it all worse, I am adding to this chaos, to the panic that has now enfolded all of us ...

And then, from far away, there arises something, a strength and a certainty, and as it does, the chaos lessens slightly, the pain recedes enough for me to try and focus, try and struggle now towards the strength I can perceive, and there, and there, oh thank the powers of the Universe, there is a master, there is a Docem, there is someone coming to protect me, hold me steady, make me still.

My relief is such that it takes some time to realise just who it is I'm clinging to in such desperation and such gratitude; and when I do I am astonished for the Docem who has come is Mark, it is my brother and yet, this is never who my brother was, this is a new one, a different one, and as I align and calm within his steady fields of midnight blue, I begin to understand what happened here and that what we had waited for had finally arrived.

Memory Decisions

I regain my composure slowly and phase back into myself, until I become aware that I am on the floor of the reception room and there is an uproar of disturbance of a different kind, of a crass and painful kind – oh my Lord, here are the human potentials, and they are scared, so scared, my two are terrified of me, and terrified for me in equal measure, they are connected to me and they must have seen and felt so many things that they should never had to have experienced at this delicate state of their unfoldments.

I seek for Satari, and we link together strongly and together, we weave a mesh of silence and tranquillity to fall across the room, to calm things down, to give us time to regain our presences and faculties.

We're not doing it very well, we are both too out of balance and too weak, but even the effort produces a noticeable drop in the disturbances and that in turn makes it easier to go back to try and strengthen the mesh, make it more coherent and cohesive.

It is then that we feel a lifting wave of powerful support, a groundswell rising that flows through us and raises us, high and higher still, until Satari and I are high above the mesh and in a timeless space of clarity, of deep control.

"Mark?" I enquire hesitantly, and when the wave becomes an aspect of a much greater being, a much greater power altogether I apologise and give a formal greeting as is right and proper, "Markus Edwards, my Lord and Docem, I thank you for your assistance."

Satari similarly sends her deep respect and gratitude, and for the first time, we now hear our master's voice as he responds with a message of acceptance of our obedience to his leadership that is loving, short and entirely sufficient to have all thoughts of my brother Mark who played with me and cared for me, disintegrate and in its place, the other was, the alpha and omega, as though it always was that way, and could not be but be that way, from now until forever.

He draws us closer, brings us nearer and makes us one; and so as one we first of all bring calm and beauty, and a deepening of sleep to our poor Arada who have suffered much from the disturbance. He decides that they should not forget, but simply sleep for now and that what had been absolutely an unfoldment would be part of theirs in every way; and so we soothe them, and we love them, more and more until they're all asleep and healed and smiling in their deepest dreams.

Then he takes us to the human potentials, and here he offers us a choice – we are Cestra, and the highest ranking ones within his house, new though it may be.

Do we want to take their memories of the events, and simply go on as though nothing happened here at all that was the least bit out of the ordinary, or do we want to explain and have them retain all or some level of what it feels like to be in a house when at the same time, the resident Docem transcends to Ferata and her Cestra consort becomes the new Docem?

I make my decision on behalf of my potentials right away. They are immaculate and innocent, immensely pure and virtually unwritten; I find that intoxicatingly attractive and I feel that to retain a sense of the events would not be any kind of benefit.

My Lord Markus follows my reasoning and acknowledges my decision; I feel a strange sense of pride, of being grown up and important when he does and I am delighted. With Lady Adela, I always felt like such a child, so clumsy, useless, pointless and no matter how gentle and profound her love for me should be, I never had the sense that I was anything of any consequence at all.

Satari is not as immediately sure as I was; but eventually, she too decides to have them forget. Our Lord acknowledges her decision in the same sober and respectful way and moves towards the potentials, begins the processes of re-alignment when I cannot help but call to him, "But what of the other one, my Lord? What of your own potential?"

He stops dead in mid space and for just one fleeting moment, I recognise the old Mark as I knew him, before our new Docem re-establishes himself.

He requests that I should look after his potential and accept him into my group; that I should care for him until the festival and then, with what might just appear an afterthought if we had not been all so very close, he swiftly states that his potential should remain untouched.

Satari notes, "This will cause a considerable incongruency, my Lord."

Our Docem pauses, then addresses me directly. "Alexandra, are you willing to devote the extra time and attention this course of action would entail?"

I am a little shocked that he should choose to entrust me with the well being of his own potential, and not Satari, who is older than I am and more experienced in every way. I can feel that she is somewhat saddened by this but not too surprised; I think she always had her doubts about becoming first and consort to our brother when he was still a Cestra, just like us.

"I am, my Lord," I answer him and behind the formal statement lies a further qualification, "And I am honoured by your trust in me, and your request."

"So it will be."

Our Docem is very strong, very focussed, very new and bright; to be with him, to be a part of him as he engages with the times and shapes of the potential's memories, laid down in strands and waves of pulses, already fully now a structural reality inside their very beings, is an excitement, is a delight. He knows exactly what he is doing, and he does it beautifully; at the same time, he takes each one and then again, together as a group, enfolds the human servants too with consummate ease into his web and starts to undo their memories, just as one might wipe away a message written with a lipstick on a mirror, a letter at a time, starting from the back.

Quite soon, there is a nothing from before the moment when our now transcended Lady Adela entered this room; and he replaces that with an entrance of himself alone, and the introductions are to him, instead of her.

When time has moved back into sync with where we are, he throws a tracing web to check for incongruencies – there are many little things, mentions of the Lady, her name on the invitations, the sense and feeling of her in the house upon arrival, all of that changes materially and for the innocent potentials, it was now just as though all that had never been.

We traverse the new insertions one more time and they are smooth and beautiful.

Satari and I both sigh with pleasure at this task so wonderfully accomplished and our Docem too is pleased, with him, with us, and now he tells us that he needs a time to be alone and settle in, perhaps to sleep, and gives us watch and guard to finish the proceedings of this night.

We are proud and happy to be given such responsibility and wish him joy in restoration; we send him our admiration and our love and he takes it readily, he needs it well enough and though he doesn't say or think, I think we know that he is not as strong or centred yet than he would have to show us, and himself.

I have to smile.

Being Docem must be quite a task.

I frankly cannot wait until I find out for myself.

Potential

When I return to my place in the drawing room, and take up station and attention just one moment before the tracing mesh is merging into now, all is calm, and quiet.

My two potentials, Richard and Royce, are wide eyed, wide open and excited about being here, about learning more of me and of my kind, and I am struck again by their sheer youth, their innocence and by their power.

They are truly glorious, fine human beings, delicious and entirely uncomplicated; this is what I like about a human, to me, this is in essence who they are supposed to be. If I want complications and incredible unfoldments, I would look to others of my own kind, not theirs.

In that way I am different from Mark – Lord Markus, now - and from Satari too. And that is pleasing just as well, for one might think that being so inordinately intertwined with others as we are, it would be possible to lose a sense of self, and merge into this group identity but that is not the case for me.

I still like my humans raw and clean, just like I always have. These two here are outstandingly beautiful men, outstandingly attractive and their existing matrix needs so little in the way of work or polish, for they shine quite brightly as they are.

I like them as a brace as well; in short, I love them and I love the way they make me feel. I find it easy to retain a good balance between my interest and to be able to control that too; once, I had picked a young woman and I got so close to her that I had to seek help from Mark to stop me from engaging in an outside union which would have been a most terrible disgrace for me and for my house.

But I was very young back then and learned my lesson from this; the trick is to not to need, but want, and that's a very different thing indeed.

These two, I want them and they feel that, know that and it makes them bright and shiny in response. We have been together on quite a few occasions, and they have already learned the things that they should know before the festival. This evening was supposed to be a simple routine, a ceremonial ending to our preparations, and to give my Docem the opportunity to check my work, correct my work if they should notice an omission or an error on my part.

That is the theory, the fact is that the Lady Adela really didn't do a thing and didn't care for all my time here in this house, and it was always left to Mark to make suggestions, give me help or direct my attention to something that wasn't quite as it should be. I remember this fondly; he was a wonderful brother to me and I don't think I quite understood just how much all of us had then relied on him, how much of what in truth should be the Docem's work and charge was being done by him.

Lord Markus protected us, and he must have further acted to protect Adela and her movements towards her own future.

I tune out towards him.

Our new Docem is asleep and he is dreaming.

All is well with him, and I am glad.

But now, I must go and find his potential; it has been quite some time and no-one has come specifically to help him out. He must be in a state of some considerable disturbance.

I call to Satari in voice and gesture, and explain to my potentials that I have an errand that is urgent at this hour; I ask Satari to host the meeting and to have my gentlemen join with her group. Of course, they are both horrified and do not want me to be gone; I am regretful too for I won't see them now, perhaps not ever, but who is to know?

They kiss my hand with fervour and with reverence; I wish them well and take my leave.

I find the last potential in the corridor before the entrance to the Underworld. He is sitting on the floor, with his head in his hands, in total dissolution and entirely unaware of my approach, or of my presence.

He is crying, hard.

I go to him and understand that I must be completely physical to reach him and to give the first and most important safety anchor, long before more subtle means to steady and to heal him may then be employed; so I make sure I am and then I kneel beside him, take his wrists with my hands, pull them away from his face and speak to him, "Can you hear me? Are you alright?"

He focuses on my with difficulty and it is difficult for me to feel his pain, to see him like this, but he most clearly needs my help and my discomfort is of no concern right at this moment.

"Who are you?" he says hoarsely, "Where is Edwards? He's dead, isn't he. Edwards is dead ..."

I have to fight against the onslaught of loss and desolation from him, I cannot side step this or dematerialise without losing the physical contact, so instead, I move forward and take him in my arms, draw him to me and he wraps himself around me, holds me tight, and he is trembling.

"Shhh," I say into his hair, close to his ear, "He isn't dead, it's alright, everything is alright now."

The potential whose name I don't remember draws back so he can see my face. He is disbelieving, but he has heard me and is trying to understand.

"He was here," he says urgently, "He was right here, and then something – happened. Something happened to him. Something terrible happened to him ..."

I squeeze his shoulders and shake him lightly to keep him focussed on the here and now.

"Something did happen," I say carefully and clearly. "He transformed, ascended. He is the Docem now. That's why you can't feel him where he was before, because he isn't there anymore. He has moved."

The potential takes a deep breath, moves back and out of my touch, leans up against the wall and drops his head back.

"He's not dead?" he asks again.

"He's not dead. He is right here, just up there ..." I point to the stairwell behind us, "He is in his rooms, sleeping, resting."

The potential looks past me down the corridor. He sighs again and seems to step down from his state of confusion a little more. He looks back to me. "Who are you?" he asks, "Why are you here, and not ..."

I nod because of course, what we are doing here is highly unconventional, if even if it isn't a direct breach of the Covenant.

"I am Alexandra," I tell him, "I am a Cestra here, the same as – " I try and can't say it like that, so I have to use the correct form and continue, " ... the same as my Lord Markus, who is now our Docem, was when you first met him. Not as experienced of course, but I am Cestra, and he has asked me to care for you and make sure you are alright, until the festival."

"What happened to the other one? Lady Adela? Where is she?"

"She has gone away," I say, and there is only a fleeting sadness there, just for one moment I allow myself to feel the emptiness of that place where my Lady had been as long as I have been alive in my new being here. This place will always remain empty now. She has left it, she has left us for the stars, the mountains and the trees.

The potential watches me and in doing so, he calms more still as he asks, "Has she died?"

I shake my head and smile.

"No, of course not! She has ascended to Ferata. Did – he – not tell you about these things?"

He shakes his head and sighs again, heavily. "We hardly talked at all," he says, very sadly. "A few sentences, that's all. He was about to show me something, something to do with this mirror, and then ..." He shakes his head and puts his hands before his eyes again. I move swiftly.

"Here," I say and sit down beside him. "What is your name?"

"My name's Burrows. Steve. Steve Burrows."

I hold out my hand to him and say, "Will you let me take care of you, Steve Burrows? As my Lord Markus wants me to?"

He looks deeply into my eyes and something passes between us, something strange and unusual, something that I am not used to feeling from a human; it was more as though he was already of our kind in some peculiar way. I am quite struck by this and cannot think to speak or move; but then, he nods and takes my hand, squeezes it cautiously and say, "Yes, Alexandra. I will."

I am curiously touched by his submission and his willingness to trust me. It is not an easy thing for him; he has suffered much tonight and I begin to see just why my Lord should go out of his way at this late stage for this one. There are great depths to him, a great many strands of different flavours, but I get a sense that there is something deep below all that which would be exquisite if it could be known.

A tingle spreads throughout my systems and I find that I have stepped into an even tighter presence, am defining even more profoundly here in physicality, as though he is drawing me down and into his own realm, a feeling that is most surprising and never yet experienced.

This one is a true potential, has a potential that makes me understand the meaning of the term in a very different way.

I look down at his hand that still is in mine, a bridge connection between two beings who I always thought were of essential different kinds, but here with him, I'm not so sure that this is strictly true, and this confuses me entirely.

I withdraw my hand and smile, a little nervously.

"You should rest," I say and rise. He looks up at me and the sensation is gone; he is just a tired potential, an innocent who has seen more and felt far more than should have been the case and has been left like driftwood in the process, lost and helpless, without roots or nourishment, on a far and alien shore.

I smile and hold out my hand to him again. He smiles tiredly in return, shakes his head and gets to his feet, loses his balance and holds on to the wall so he won't fall.

"Come with me," I say and take his free arm, place it over my shoulder. It is hot, vibrant through the fabric of his suit, and he is noticeably trembling from the effort. I want to send him some strength, some extra energy but I don't think that is allowed; he is not yet Arada and I have no idea what such exchanges at this stage would cause to happen. I'm not willing to make a mistake through unknowingness, so I simply use my physical strength to start walking him towards the stairs.

Oh! But it has been a long, long time since such I've engaged! It was old and new, different and very peculiar, all at the same time.

The stairs prove to be quite a challenge, but he seems to recover and find reserves of strength within himself as we go; on the first floor landing, I make the decision to put him in my room instead of one of the many, many empty rooms elsewhere in the house.

With only four of us, we all slept here on the first floor; now, there's only three. I'm sure that in the larger houses the arrangements would be far more formal, and perhaps they will be once our new Docem has moved us and has built up his own house.

For now, we are right here and I take the potential – Steve, I must remember his name – to my own rooms which lie at the end of the corridor. Before the door of what used to be my brother Mark's rooms, I pause us and I tell him, "Lord Markus is in there. This is where he is sleeping."

"Can I see him?" the potential asks, and I consider his request.

It would be good for him to really be aware that Lord Markus was very much still with us, simply changed; he cannot feel him yet and is most likely looking in all the wrong places as well. Yet my Lord needs his rest and furthermore, I have no idea just what kind of manifestation he would have chosen for his sleep.

Seeing him in some inhuman state would not alleviate the potential's fear or confusion, and so I decide and say, "No, not yet. He is resting and he needs his rest." The potential is crestfallen, so I add, "You know how this has affected you, and you are only on the far outside of these events. His own Lady has ascended this night, and he has undergone a great transformation; he has been inside of it all, a part of it. We must give him time to re-establish."

The potential frowns and nods. He says, "Of course. How stupid of me. I hadn't thought of it like that. I'm sorry, I ... didn't think. Of course, he must not be disturbed ..."

So we move along, past what used to be the rooms of Lady Adela and that gives me the strangest sense of vertigo again, so much so that I feel the need to lean on the potential for a moment. He is surprised but picks up from his end and so we mostly lean on one another.

Thus we arrive in my room.

It is dark and that is soothing to my senses and to my being. I guide us both to the bed, and we simply get on it and lie in the darkness, and not a little while later we turn to each other and embrace, for comfort and for presence.

It is then that his tiredness and loss, his confusion and his fear becomes as a fire to me that warms me, gives me center, gives me purpose, and I in turn become the night to surround him, star blessed and radiant, so he may sleep, and rest.

A Journey Of Discovery

To lie with a sleeping human for an entire night is an experience I have never had before. It was very strange, exotic and unsettling; it called within me elder states and memories I had not sought to access in a long time.

I stroked him with care, dispersed gathering storm clouds and generally kept him safe, and later, warm. To observe his system responding to the changes in the night was fascinating, a journey of discovery that was tremendous and it did set me to wonder why it was that we were so forbidden to have any contact with these at all, and if we did, just why the rules and regulations that existed were so strict and did preclude precisely this kind of intimate learning I was experiencing here.

As the night moved to its zenith and the world became a shifted place of magic and of resonance, and as Satari also sought to find her restoration and began to drift away, I was left alone, the guardian of the house.

Extraordinary.

We do not sleep as humans do, and usually for different reasons; I cannot recall a time when I was so alone, and so responsible, and for so many!

But it was attractive too, and very satisfying. I placed myself in a position where I could feel them all, observe them all and know when something needed a response – a re-assurance, an adjustment, or a simple sense that they were not alone.

The Arada were well and dreaming their own dreams.

My Lord was vibrant, even in his sleep; and I began to wonder just how long he would remain in this condition. Sleep can last for a very long time with our kind and the festival was only four days away now. This troubled me deeply. To interrupt a sleeper was frowned upon for it can easily destroy the tender new connections and the subtle fine attunements that occur; and those were ordinary circumstances, when my Lord Markus was far more likely to be trying to restore most all of him right from the inside out.

This house was in deep disarray.

It really was much worse than first I had imagined or foreseen.

Just how many laws had we broken between us in a single night?

The thought makes me shiver and I use the potential to ground myself in my guard duties once more, and I make an effort not to think too much and simply drift into the guardian state, responding as and when and resting in between.

He awoke towards the zenith of the day, slow stretching and awareness rising, a fascinating thing and strikingly similar to the way we phase in and out of material manifestation, only here it was disguised by his existing body that took all the attention and gave the illusion that he was only one thing, all the time.

Eventually, he opened his eyes into the comparative brightness of the room and focussed on me, lying next to him and thus, he startled backwards into full awareness.

He moved away from me, sat up rapidly, moved further away until he was at the edge of the bed and then, when I did neither move nor speak, just smiled a little re-assurance, he rubbed his face in his hands, rubbed his hands through his hair and sighed, then coughed.

"How are you feeling?" I ask him quietly and remain quite still as not to frighten him with movement and to make it clear that he is safe, that nothing will befall him here, and that my role is that of someone who is here to help, not harm.

He looks down at himself as though that would inform him of the answer to my question. He is still wearing all his clothes from the night before, very crumpled they are, but it gives him a relief to know that nothing untoward did happen in the night, something that he might not know or now remember, but that happened, nonetheless.

Then he looks back to me and smiles, cautiously. He has a lovely smile. It transforms his face, his features, and I respond by smiling far more deeply in return.

"Alright," he says, "Hungry. Hungry as hell."

For a moment, I am completely confused. He notices this and stops smiling immediately. I am sorry. I am supposed to take care of you, make you feel at ease. I'm not doing a very good job. He is nervous again, unsure again, and I am not handling this situation as I should be.

"I am sorry," I say and I marvel how long it must have been since last I had to use that choice of words with anyone at all, "I'm sorry. I forgot about ... your eating. I will arrange something right away. What would you like to – eat?"

He shrugs his shoulders nervously. "It doesn't matter," he says, "It's ok, I'll be on my way. I can get something at home, don't worry about it."

Again, I am shocked and confused. He is leaving? Is he supposed to leave? I realise that in guarding him through the night I must have assumed that he is somehow of this house, that he was here to stay, that he was – well, one of us!

Now, I am lost and I don't know how to proceed.

What would my Lord Markus want me to do under the circumstances?

The potential hasn't been told anything. He hasn't been prepared. He has been witness to extremely sensitive and intimate events in our house and he is unstable. I feel instinctively that he shouldn't leave, but can I stop him? What is the procedure in this situation? What am I to do?

I reach out for my Lord but he is far away and only just the faintest resonance connection is remaining. Even if I was to call him, was to wake him which indeed would be a questionable choice of action, it would take time for him to re-assemble and emerge.

Is this an emergency?

The potential is becoming ever more uncertain and unsure because I am not answering and he can feel that I am getting more and more dismayed.

What am I to do?

I don't know. I am beginning to feel a sensation rising in me that at first I simply do not recognise, and then I do – I am afraid, and I am panicking. In all the years I've spent in this house, this has never happened. There has always been someone to take care of me, to show me what to do or to stabilise me well before such a disturbance should ever get to the point it is now present and within me.

I am spinning too fast in my center and it is getting worse.

The potential has now decided that there is something wrong, and he cautiously leans further towards me, extends a tentative hand towards me and he says, "Lady? Alexandra? Are you alright? Is there something wrong?"

The first law is that of love. This does not guide me here. The second rule is of unfoldment. There are more than one, his, but also mine. My unfoldments are in danger in this situation and need help. My Lord Markus told me that he didn't want this one to not remember, and that surely means that he has plans for this potential; and I don't know if it is wrong or right, or a transgression, but I call upon the human then to give me aid and comfort.

"I don't know what I should do," I tell him, and the relief is instant, and enormous. Some of the energy I held inside my center is released and so I speak on, fast, to hasten this most welcome process, "I was told to care for you, but my Lord Markus did not give any detailed instructions. I don't know if I am supposed to keep you here or let you leave, and I am failing in my duty of care towards you. This is all unknowable, and I can't think of any guidelines I should follow."

The potential receives my stream of distress and information with surprise but strangely, seems to calm all through it; when I am finished, he leans a little further towards me and says, "I'm not sure what's going on here, but this looks like ... it's like in war, when all the officers have died, and left a junior in charge. Is that what's happened here?"

I nod with relief that he understands my situation, and with more relief that I have not materially contributed to his confusion by deciding to tell him about my circumstances. He nods in return and says, "Isn't there someone you can call? Your headquarters? For new orders?"

I am confused and the spinning sensation begins again. This time, I speak my thoughts out aloud right away. "The Docem is who is in charge, there is no-one else. Only if one should be lost, or there is a catastrophe, there is a place where we were told to go. But if I go there, I declare our house has fallen, and it has not, and that wouldn't be true, and I don't know what would happen then ..."

The potential makes a gesture and stops me from going any further. He leans forward and cautiously reaches out and takes my hand in his. I can make it so that he will have something he can touch and feel only just in time, but this small act of will and of control helps me, it helps me right away, and I feel better.

He looks at my hand, then into my eyes and says with a very small smile, "I guess it wouldn't help to tell you to breathe, would it."

His smile transmits to me and I smile in return. "No, indeed, that wouldn't help at all."

"Alright," he says and the pressure he places around my fingertips increases noticeably, a warming sensation that travels up my arm, into my shoulder and from there streams into my head and down towards my center, bringing soothing and clarity as it goes.

"Alright," he says, "Now, let's be calm and think about the situation."

I must have given him a flash of my former fears returning for he says rapidly, "First of all, don't worry about me. I'm alright. I'm here, I'm feeling ok, and I can really get my own breakfast. Ok?" He bends forward to catch my eye because I have hung my head in shame at the mention of all of that, and doubly so as he is taking care of me, when it should absolutely be the other way around.

"I don't know the first thing of how you people organise yourselves, or anything to do with you, but look," he continues in a manner designed to calm and steady me, "In every situation there are priorities. The important things. We see to those first, and the other stuff can wait until later." I nod as he speaks for that makes sense, and I await what he will tell me next, wide open. The man who is holding my hand, the human -oh my Lord, what a transgression I have initiated here! It is unconscionable! – watches me with great care for a moment, before he speaks on. "What needs to be done to keep everything running smoothly until Edwards wakes up?"

I think hard about his question and then have an answer for him.

"First of all, the Arada need to be cared for. That's the most important thing of all."

"Ok," he says and nods, "And do you know how to do that?"

It is my turn to nod. "Oh yes," I tell him positively, "I have cared for the Arada for a long time. I know what to do. And then, there's Satari to help as well. I don't have to do it alone."

"Satari? That is the other – Lady – I saw downstairs last night? The small Asian girl with the long black hair?"

"Yes, that's right. She is my senior."

"Where is she now?" he asks.

"She is asleep. She was much disturbed by last night's events and had to take care of not just her own potentials, but mine as well."

The human in the crumpled suit, half kneeling on my bed, nods and lets go off my hand. "Have you had any sleep? And, by the way, do I call you Lady Alexandra?"

A small laugh escapes me. This situation is absolutely preposterous. I am being guided by a human who doesn't know the first thing about anything at all.

"Please," I say and have to give another small giggle against my will, "Just Alexandra. The title of Lady or of Lord refers to only the Docem. And no, I have not yet rested."

He nods at that and then he says with a great deal of poise and conviction that enters me and resonates within me very well, "Alexandra, you need to rest. I'm sure you too were much disturbed by those events, and you are the youngest here from what I can see. Wake up the other one, let her take care of the ... ahm, " – "Arada", I fill in for him.

"Let her take care of those, and you must get some rest."

I think about his proposition. The Arada can be left for a long time if that should be necessary. There would be no need to disturb Satari; I too could go to sleep if there was someone left to guard the house.

"But what of you," I ask him. "I was told to look after you."

He puts his head to one side and says, "I know for a fact that Edwards could read my mind. Can you?"

Before I know it, I have nodded already. I cannot exactly read his mind, but I can know his state of mind, his moods and I can know his purposes. Young as I am, a human cannot lie to me.

He says, "I really am alright. More than that. I feel better than I have in a long time, and I'm sure that is due to you and your good care. I am offering my services. Go to sleep, and I will stand guard. I promise to wake you should anything out of the ordinary happen."

He is telling the truth. It would be a possibility. And he is right, I didn't realise how badly I need to rest and to internalise all that has happened, all that is happening still to my house. I yearn for rest and that desire rises so strongly inside me that I nearly fade away on the spot.

I look at him again, reach out in every way and although I know that I probably shouldn't, I make my decision.

PART 2

1: Steve Burrows, Guardian Assay

Doors Unlocked

Diary Entry: Saturday, December 17th. Am left guarding nest of Vampires in Central London.

I stand before the young vampire's bed in her rooms. I have received my instructions, and I have closed the curtains around her massive four poster bed on which I spent the night with her.

The material of the curtains is extraordinary.

It is completely flexible but made of many layers of very strange materials; the inner layer is opalescent white, like a cinema screen but soft and silky. I walk around the bed and enclose it entirely in these curtains that seem to seal themselves together where they meet and fuse; creating an effect like an oxygen tent.

As soon as I have fused the final set of curtains, two things happen at the same time.

The temperature in the room seems to fall through the floor in an instant; and light begins to play behind the curtains, northern lights of great intensity, they must be, or else I wouldn't be able to see this through the many-layered curtain materials and furthermore, there is the bright light of day streaming in through the bay windows.

As it gets cold, and colder still, it also becomes quieter in the room, more silent, more peaceful – it is now that I really begin to appreciate just how upset the young vampire Lady must have been, and how much her upset had disturbed the atmosphere.

I take a deep breath and when I exhale, I am astonished to see my breath creates a cloud of steam. It doesn't just feel cold, it really is cold in here now.

Amazing.

I stand and watch the lights play green and blue, white, hints of rose and saffron behind the closed curtains for a while and then it seems that they are settling down, dimming down, fading away – she must have gone to sleep.

And that leaves me in charge of all of them.

It's the most extraordinary thing, and I stand getting cold and colder still and it is my own growling stomach that startles me out of it.

I draw the heavy velveteen drapes across the bay windows overlooking a completely ordinary London street below, traffic is mild, a few people walking, the sun is shining brightly outside.

It is a splendid blue winter day, dry and pleasant.

And I am left guarding a nest of vampires.

Quietly, I withdraw from the room and close the door softly behind me, even though I am pretty sure she wouldn't hear me if I screamed and shouted and threw the furniture around; the corridor outside is much warmer and for a moment, I lean against the wall and try to collect myself.

As I look down the corridor, it occurs to me that Edwards is behind that door, just down there, the first one on this floor.

I have to see him.

I have to.

I can't not.

I hope it won't hurt him, or that no bad things will happen because of this, but there is no way I can be here and not at least try and see him.

There is a connection between me and him that is – so deep, so intense, so powerful, I can't override it with reservations about propriety or good behaviour.

I understand completely that this is most likely because of something he did to me, back at the exhibition, out in the rainy street or perhaps when I went to see him later here, that he did some thing to me that has caused this extraordinary obsession I have with him, but knowing that doesn't make it any less powerful, any less overriding.

I begin to walk down the corridor, very, very quietly, and so I come to stand before his door. It is just the same as all the doors here, old wood, strong and polished to perfection, inlaid with little art nouveau swirls, a polished brass door knob.

It's extraordinary that they should not even lock their doors; they really aren't worried about vampire hunters or villagers with stakes, that much is clear.

Cautiously, I touch the doorknob and it is so extremely cold that it burns my hand.

I shake my shirt sleeve down my arm and use it to open the door.

It is dark inside but even from the doorway, what I see takes my breath away.

The curtains around Edward's bed are not drawn.

There is no man lying on that bed.

It is untouched, completely made up.

The room is freezing.

There is a soft sheen of crystal frost on everything – and all of that reflects Edwards, and he is a galaxy, slowly swirling beneath the high ceiling in the center of the room.

I stare up at the spiral of lights that exists in its own surrounding space with diamond glittering, flashing lights and I have never seen anything so beautiful, anything so extraordinary, anything so spectacular nor anything remotely as alien as that.

It is Edwards.

This is his true form, this is what he is when he is fast asleep and dreaming.

I back out from the room, back across the threshold and pull the door to behind me.

In the corridor, I take a few more steps back and I stare at the door but what I see is the galaxy, an image indelibly burned into my mind, into my soul.

Empty

In the kitchen downstairs, I lean heavily upon the polished slate work surface and try to get some perspective on myself, on this situation.

There is no food in this kitchen.

There are absolutely no utensils of any kind.

All the cupboards are entirely empty.

There are no cleaning materials, there is no toaster, no kettle and none of the electric appliances are even connected. This kitchen was installed and has never been used, not once, not ever.

For some reason, that brings the alienness of these people closer to me, closer to home, it makes it far more real than seeing that thing upstairs, that what Edwards is when he does not walk the rainy streets of London, dressed in the disguise of a man.

I try to think and organise these disjointed images and pieces of information in my mind. But it is too much, and I can't begin to think of Edward's vampire mistress, this unbelievable creation, not a creature, that I saw last night here in the drawing room.

I leave the kitchen which is not a kitchen but just an empty shell, a pretence of a kitchen behind and make my way to the drawing room.

It is empty, there is not a trace of the events of last night, it has been cleared and cleaned to perfection.

Slowly, I walk across the deep green golden carpet to the corner table where Edwards and I had been sitting, and there I find something that stabilises me immensely – there are two pale white crescent moon shaped marks on the highly polished mahogany table, clearly visible water marks. I knew I was making them when I put my champagne glass there. I know what French polishing entails, and I know about the preciousness of these fragile antique tables. My parents had those in the family home, and it was one of the many ways I fought my endless guerrilla war against them.

Two small water marks.

It happened.

I had been here.

90

It was real and I was not insane.

It was as it was, and it was all true.

Now, what was I to do?

I pulled out the chair in which Edwards had been sitting and let myself sink down into it. I felt light headed and sick, and that gave me a clear thought to hang on to – low blood sugar, I must get something to eat.

I look up at the windows. I can't leave here. I promised Alexandra I would stay here and stand guard. I'm babysitting. You can't pop out, even for a cup of coffee, if you're babysitting.

Hell.

That's when I get up to start exploring the house, and I find a pleasant sitting room at the back, overlooking the garden, and it has a large four seater sofa, comfortable arm chairs and even a TV and some video equipment, which I find surprising, and then I find the office, and there are the monitors for the surveillance cameras covering any angle at the front, in the entrance, around the back in the walled garden, and a telephone.

I feel an extreme sense of relief when I pick up the telephone and hear the dialling tone, and even more so when I ring my own home number and am rewarded shortly after with hearing my own voice, from a time way back when, saying, "Don't talk to me unless you have something worth saying. So don't leave a message unless ..." There's the beep and I say, "Galaxy," before putting the phone down.

The phone works, there is no weird dialling out procedure. I can order a pizza.

I sit down in the chair before the surveillance cameras and laugh for a while, with my head in my hands. I'm going crazy. Yeah. I'm going to order a pizza and some coffee. I'll do that first.

The desk and the room in general doesn't seem to contain any paper. There is no printer or anything remotely relating to bills, or invoices or any kind of normal human activity. There are no pens, and this office is clearly no more an office than the kitchen is a kitchen, or Edwards is a human being.

Damn ...

I check the pocket of my brand new tuxedo, and find the credit card I put in there just in case I needed a taxi on the night or something. Then I dial directory enquiries, who helpfully provide me with the phone number of the nearest Pizza Palace. They deliver coffee. I moisten my fingertip to draw the number on the wooden desk, and dial swiftly and before the traces have faded.

I end up ordering half their menu and when that's done, I make my way to the front door to see if I can get that steel safety door open to let in the delivery. There is a manual override; I will be able to get to my pizza, chicken legs and coffee when it arrives.

That gives me a great sense of relief.

Back in the office and watching the monitors, I search around for any clues or information, but there is nothing. There is a computer, and it is connected to the Net, but I can't get into any of the files, the whole thing is locked and password protected.

Vampires surf?

I shake my head and refuse to try and imagine what kind of passwords they would use. Their birthdays. Tenth of February, 1209 …

I sit back in the chair and watch the monitors.

People are walking by the house, totally oblivious of what they're passing by.

I think of the vampire girl, Alexandra.

She was scared half to death that she was doing something wrong. Scared of Edwards? She was also so … so devoted to authority. She was looking for leadership so badly that she even took it from me, and that really threw me for a moment when I noticed that, upstairs there on her bed. She was following her orders. I wondered if that was who she used to be, when she was still a real young woman and before she joined this – oh man, this what is this, what have I let myself in for?

The amount of control Edwards had and has over me is something else. I can't fight that, it is – just complete possession. I have always wanted to be free, wanted to be me – is this whole vampire deal just a great big leap from the frying pan into the fire? Am I too going to become a mindless slave to Edwards and others like him, shitting myself in case I make a mistake or don't follow my orders correctly, at the mercy of just anyone at all who offers a command, a structure, gives an order?

And then I think, is it worth it to one day, become a galaxy when I'm asleep?

When I do, I see it again, I feel it again and I know deep inside that anything would be worth that, anything at all.

I would give myself up completely and be Edward's slave for as long as it took, if that's what it would take to be like that, experience what it was like to be – that.

It is a strange sensation to realise that about me.

It is a complete 180' u-turn on all I ever held to be true, held to be holy.

I don't know me at all.

I never did.

But I was right on one count.

Here was a chance to find out the truth – if I was brave enough to face it.

Underworld

I ate my pizza in the garden.

It was walled all around, very high, but big enough to still have a small pool of sunlight left from the low, small, golden winter sun this day.

There were a lot of strange plants, and some were in flower even this late in the year, small orange blossoms on fine, black twisted stems that caught dew drops in their angles and made the bush sparkle.

I sat down on a wet stone bench and enjoyed the sensation of the cold penetrating into my buttocks, reminding me that I was here, that I was alive.

I ate and drank the coffee, and I could hear the sounds of the city far away behind the walls, and I could feel the reality of all of that receding more with every heartbeat, and a stillness coming to me, a satisfaction, yes, perhaps even a joy at this day, being in this place.

I remained there until the sun sank below the level of the western wall and it became very cold. I wondered what it would be like to be here and not feel this cold, to be able to remain here in stillness and wonder until the first stars of night would begin to unveil themselves against the orange glow of the city lights, and simply to be here and watch them move across the sky, until the dawn would come and a new day would rise before my tireless and immortal eyes.

The thought made my still human eyes fill with tears of longing and of gratitude both.

Slowly and stiffly, I rose and collected the remains of my dinner, those incongruent cardboard boxes with their green and red print and empty polystyrene cups, items that did not belong here, not in this garden, not in this house, and it was those items that were anachronistic and of the past, when the old house itself and all the life here in this garden was of now, and of the future.

I listened with all my senses when I stepped back into the kitchen, but the house was silent and very still, dreaming and restful, welcoming, beckoning me to join in this, to lie down and enter into this festival of peace, and of silence.

But once again, my otherness was brought back to me with sharp and shock when I collided painfully in the dark with the corner of one of the work units, dropped what I was carrying and hardly stifled a cry in time.

I was freezing, my hip hurt like hell and I was me again.

No timeless vampire, no welcome guardian, powerful and strong, I was not a member of this place, not at all.

I was just a man, a human, and me at that, which made it worse.

I felt my way to a light switch by the kitchen door and turned on the lights. The blue white artificial brightness exploded around me with such violence, it blinded me and by the time I had recovered from that, the pain in my hip had receded somewhat and I was suitably humbled in all ways.

Now, I need the bathroom.

In the bathroom mirror, I stare at myself for the longest time. I look terrible. Pale, gaunt, big shadows under my eyes like bruises. My hair is a mess, a full day's stubble doesn't help. The shirt I'm wearing is crumpled, so is the suit.

I am crumpled.

I take some time to sort myself out, wash, run my hands through my hair with water to control it to some extent, then I wander back through the house, aimlessly.

At one point, I come across the corridor behind the stairs, the one that terminates in the huge golden mirror, the one where Edwards disappeared with his mistress in a rushing storm right before my eyes.

I try and remember what happened, what happened just before that, what we were saying and doing, but it is unclear and as though every time I think about it, the pictures in my head slide like a waterfall straight back into that moment when Edwards cried out, spun around and the woman appeared right behind him, caught him in her arms and then the entire place just spun into madness, a crazy whirlpool that sucked me in, a leaf in a hurricane, and such confusion ...

I shake my head to try and clear those images, those sensations and I try to stop myself short of that moment when I felt something in all that confusion, when I felt Edwards disappearing, a tearing sensation that was horrendous, so painful that I don't have the words to begin to describe how it made me feel, and I screamed, I think I screamed ...

I have to lean against the wall and try to control my breathing.

Think. Think of before that. When you came down this corridor, with Edwards at your shoulder, and you looked into the mirror and saw only yourself.

For some reason, that makes me smile and I push myself away from the wall then and stand right in that place, in front of the mirror, and remember how he phased into the picture and how fascinated I was to observe that, from nothing into a denseness that revealed itself only by distorting the wall behind us at first, and then it became a swirling cloud that took his shape, before he was right there – brilliant bright, and absolutely real.

Why had he brought me here?

To show me the mirror trick?

I look up at the ceiling, at the walls. I back up further and go to the end of the corridor, try and work out the layout of the walls and the staircase, and then it becomes clear to me what I probably already knew subconsciously – this corridor should not be ending there.

There is more to this house, there is room behind the wall with the mirror.

The mirror is an entrance door to a secret place within this house, and that's what Edwards wanted me to see, that's what he wanted to show me.

I look into the mirror and for a moment it is as though I see him, standing next to me, immaculate and perfect, smiling.

Edwards wants me to see what is behind the mirror.

The thought becomes like a command; like a challenge and instruction; a legacy from beyond the grave.

There must be a way to get behind this mirror.

Is there a way? Or can only vampires pass through it somehow?

That can't be it, I must be able to gain entrance or he wouldn't have brought me here.

I step up close to the mirror and begin to trace the frame with my eyes, with my fingertips. It is heavily carved, deeply carved with floral interlacements and looks as though it was covered in gold leaf only yesterday afternoon, so bright and fresh does the gold look and shine.

Help me, Edwards, I think to myself.

Where is the mechanism to open this door?

I close my eyes and let my fingertips stray across the frame, no, it isn't here, it's on the other side, it's on the right, lower down, lower down – there.

My eyes snap open and I kneel down to see that my hand has found a triple interlacement of leaves that is not repeated in the pattern above, or below.

I hold my breath and place three fingers, one in the center of each leaf, and press down gently. The leaves give, softly, and deeply, they disappear into the frame and then I meet a resistance. I push harder and there is an audible click, then a whoosh as with a fast movement that frightens me and makes me pull back my hand back sharply, the entire wall slides backwards a good three feet, then slowly begins to move away and to the left, revealing a darkness, and a green glow ahead.

Into my head floats a single word, clearly defined –

Underworld.

I have found the entrance to the Underworld.

Arada

I take a deep breath, as though I can breathe the light that exists here in the corridor and it will hold out when I step across the threshold and be with me when I enter there, like a diver; then I start forward and step into the resonant darkness beyond.

I stand on a wide platform that falls off steeply and I look into an underground room that is wide and huge, huge arched ceilings reaching up to more than three times my height, and wide stairs sweeping down in a slow spiral to the ground.

Slowly, my eyes begin to adjust and I can make out shapes below, just a few in a green swirling mist that seems to glow from within, then I begin to make out other colours as well, soft, fine colours emanating from the shapes.

I won't gives these shapes the designation of "coffins" for I know, I feel that they are no such thing; and this entire beautiful room is not a vault; it is a place full of resonant life that I can sense at the furthest edges of my awareness.

Slowly, I begin to descend the stairs.

Behind me, the entrance closes softly, inaudibly. I know that it does because I can feel and see the effect of the reduction in the light as it slides back to its original position, and when the last shimmer has gone, and the vibrant dark is all there is, my attention to what I find here is complete.

I can't take my eyes of the shapes, rounded shapes, just seven, all told, in the center of the floor, in a circular arrangement, and each one contains what seems to be a sleeping human being.

A sleeping, dreaming human being.

This is the transformation in action; this is where I will be when I am chosen and have been selected to become a part of Edward's house.

I am absolutely fascinated.

The floor beneath my feet is soft and giving; slow swirling mists of subtle greens play around my feet and my footfalls are inaudible as I cautiously and reverently make for the first of these resting places, dreaming beds or altars they might be, so I might take a closer look.

Before me lies a very young woman, of perhaps 18 years of age, with long dark hair and a strong oriental flavour to her features, in a white gown that leaves her neck and arms bare. She is as beautiful as I have ever seen anyone to be.

I look at her face, her skin; her expression is one of utter calm and relaxation, with perhaps the smallest shine of a smile around her lips.

Her skin is smooth; translucent; and as I look at her, am drawn more and more to her, to want to know her, know more about her, connect with her in a deep and profound sensation of desire and longing both, I can see that she is surrounded by those soft, fine veils of colour; but no, that's not quite right and then I understand that she is both the body and the colours, that they are her, a part of her and that what I do want from her is not her body but her colours.

They are precious beyond belief.

I have always had a love for colours; it was what first attracted me to paint and brush and to materials, stone and gem, to sky and forest; night and day; these colours I perceive here are of such brilliance and purity as I have never known, they are a joy and a healing, an intoxication and a festival and I have to get closer to that, make that my own – I have to taste her ruby, her enchanted emerald and her eternal sapphire blue; I must know the touch of her splendid ultraviolet and the sensation of her gold, in my mouth, in my fingertips, inside of me.

I bend over her, and entirely overcome by my hunger for her colours, I begin to kiss them at first, touch them with my lips, with my tongue, and they come to me most willingly, and slide towards me, first the faint and sensuous opalescent white that weaves amongst them all, containing tiny starbursts of many colours in its very essence; and I nearly faint with pleasure for it tastes so good, flows inside me so readily and with such deep conviction, with compassion, wants to fill my need for what this is, my hunger, and it an old hunger, an ancient hunger that I thought would never now be stilled, would never find fulfilment and yet here it is, and it is more fantastic and more thrilling, more delicious and more available than I had ever dared to dream.

I drink hungrily then, draw this unbelievable essence of beauty and of splendour deeply right into my deepest structures, and then the colours begin to rush; first one, then another, faster, more, more richness, more depth, more desire; I have to have more, all, everything – COME TO ME!

And it comes, it all comes, a huge and glorious flood wave of everything, it arises at the far horizon, high and higher still and it comes closer, closer – I open myself to be as wide and far as all the worlds and then the wave that contains all the colours, all at once, comes crashing to me, roaring into me and I am ecstasy and then, I cease to be at all.

2: Gaius Decius Levinius, Segar

Fascination

When all hell was let loose across the community, just four days before the Festival, I was already in London, and in the right place.

I had been tuning in to the unfoldments at the house of Adela Bach since first I arrived and my amusement at the situation had grown to the degree that it breached the threshold and went to fascination.

It had been a long time indeed since I had been thus fascinated.

It was enlivening.

Chaos has a habit of being exactly that, and to be entirely truthful, I had missed a little chaos that was not strictly of my own making.

Few and rare the occasions!

But here was not just chaos, but extreme chaos, and extreme the repercussions. I decided to make the chaos worse, and put in an appearance.

That idea made me chuckle.

I have often thought that to be a Segar is a silent invitation to create chaos in a system that would otherwise be so stable, there would be no evolution at all; and then again, I thought that the kind of chaos we create is built right into the system, and therefore a part of it, and therefore no true chaos at all.

But here, at Adela Bach's house, there was randomness that had run out of control, and now the Cardor were spiralling in red and gold, tying themselves in knots undoubtedly and taking their time to consult all and every aspect of the Covenant in every combination. I laughed to myself. It might well take a couple of decades before they finally came to a decision, a conclusion and when they did, it would most likely end up being a minute fine tuning of two or three sub paragraphs of the lower Covenant.

In the meantime, the community was in uproar and Adela's young Docem was ready to tear himself to pieces and put an end to the entire line, once and for all.

I had to chuckle again.

He had been Docem for one single day, and had already the two worst crimes that could possibly be committed to his name – a rogue semi-conversion, and the extinction of one of his Arada. This must surely be a record!

It was just as well that Adela had taken the opportunity to escape into Ferata, for the shame would have been certain to put an end to her as well.

I remember Adela well. I remember her tastes with some fondness; she had been Arada in the house where I concluded my Cestra service and had significantly contributed to my recovery following my master's ascendance.

I felt a sense of kinship with her house although she wasn't of my line, and I decided to make an appearance, meet this young Docem who used to be her consort. It should be interesting, and an unusual opportunity to study a young one in such a state of shame and public dissolution.

I smiled to myself, tuned into the community, focussed on the house that lay at the very center of the storm of disturbance and disgust, and phased myself into what once had been the house of Adela Bach.

Anger

I chose to remain stepped off to observe the situation for a time.

This house, if you can even call it by this honoured designation, this house doesn't have anyone at all who has the ability to perceive at this level, even if they paid attention; as it is, they have shut down and created a safety field of exclusion around themselves, so they no longer have to hear the cries of shame and disgust, of sorrow and of disbelief that are resonating around the community like so many bells of doom will toll.

I find them all together, clinging to each other and wailing all as one in one of the upstairs bedrooms of the London townhouse that used to belong to Adela.

I hover in a corner of the ceiling and observe them with rising delight and fascination.

What a group!

Two hysterical infant Cestra girls, hardly off their Arada nests. One Docem so young, he might as well be hardly more than a fledgling Cestra himself, absolutely at sea. And the semi-conversion, a crazy half human who committed the unthinkable crime of crimes and killed an Arada on this day.

Even I am having trouble with that concept, and even though I don't particularly feel a sense of responsibility or caretaking any longer, having long outgrown my own Docem stage, I still remember what it was like to care for the beautiful dreaming ones, and I decide to check on the surviving Arada.

They are in a sorry state, lost, confused and in great pain; it is absolutely appalling and I am beginning to get angry at the young Docem for leaving these innocents in such a state.

That in and of itself is a delight to me; I haven't felt anything even approaching anger in many centuries and it is good to know that the ability is still alive and wasn't lost just simply because it was never needed, never used for such a long time.

I had quite forgotten how empowering a charge it is that bursts forth and sweeps away so many detailed considerations in preference; and so it is that I attend to the Arada with a will, feed them powerfully and dream them deeply, far more deeply than would have been at the disposal of a Docem; they will be safe now and until some form of sensible arrangement for their future unfoldments can be found.

These Arada have been severely damaged and that is inconceivable. This should never have happened at all!

At least now the young Docem has pulled himself together enough from his self pitying spirals to have noticed my presence in the house and my interventions with what should have been his responsibilities, his Arada; through him, the others become aware of me as well and I find a distaste as I am being touched by the monstrosity, the murderer. I reject his presence absolutely and slap him back; this causes the entire group to fall back as one and recede into a stunned silence.

I am still angry and I leave it be that way as I manifest explosively into their presence.

Wilderness

I shift into the room where the perpetrators of this – unknowable array of crimes, indeed! – are gathered like lightning will strike, come rushing in through the dimensions so fast and hard, into full out manifestation that it causes the very air in the room to become a storm of displacement, and their systems flail and bend in agony of nearly being torn apart.

Far away in the community, there is a satisfaction at their pain; an undertone of applause at my actions mixed in with more disbelief and shock at my own transgression of the Covenant but this is quite overwhelmed by a noticeable desire that I should cause them more pain still, that I should punish them for what they did to the Arada, to the Arada's many years and many lives, and all that was so heedlessly destroyed and taken in an instant, from all of us, indeed.

This antagonism that has never been in all the times the oldest now amongst us can remember resonates and feeds right back upon itself; shockwaves upon shockwaves travel back and forth, and with some interest I become aware that I myself am at the center of this storm, and that from here, I hold leverage over its unfoldments.

That is fascinating, indeed.

I side step into timelessness and consider the issues at hand.

I have breached the Covenant by becoming involved in the affairs of a house that isn't even of my line. Theoretically, I can be here, but only to observe and interact in a strictly limited fashion; for a Segar to take a direct hand in the basic running of another's house is unheard of.

This is however exactly what I did when, moved by my state of appalment and anger as I was, I took the decision to come to the suffering Arada's aid and act in place of Docem to stabilise their situation.

Further, I have taken action designed to inflict injury on the remaining members of this house; this is indeed a breach of the first law, and far more serious.

Chaos.

So that is what true chaos actually is, what it feels like.

This is what it is to be outside the Covenant.

I swirl for a moment and must take time to stabilise before I can go on to consider my next course of action.

This is the question – shall I return to the safety and beauty of the Covenant, or shall I remain outside of it?

It is true that until this very moment, it had never occurred to me to leave the Covenant. I had played games and amused myself in many different ways, but I had never transgressed against the central tenements of the Covenant and it is inconceivable that I should have been so easily aroused as to have done this, on this day.

It is inconceivable and yet it happened; and this is frightening.

I consider.

Is this all that lies between us and anarchy?

One thought? One feeling? One occurrence?

Is that all it takes to make a hundred thousand years of civilisation and co-operation simply disappear as though it had never been?

And as I consider these issues and look to all the knowledge and understanding, my evidence and experience, it comes to me that this very question is indeed what heralds the beginning of my transformation from Segar, The One Who Walks Alone, to Cardor, The Lawmaker.

I could never truly understand what being Cardor was about, or why one should ever want to go to the place they went, and do the things they did, whatever those things might be; I was happy to explore the worlds and to be drawn from one fascination to the next, enjoying myself tremendously and being quite incapable of even understanding why this extraordinary state of freedom should ever end at all.

Here it is.

I become unsteady for a moment and phase this way and that in timelessness, and as I do, I understand the Covenant and our ways of being in a different way, from a different perspective.

Perhaps it is impossible to know a thing unless you are outside of it as well?

I have stepped outside the Covenant, and now, it is up to me what I should choose.

In breaking the First Law, I broke them all and now, they are all broken; I acted in anger and in vengeance and inflicted pain on these which are but children and should have been in my compassion, just the same as the Arada they had so bitterly neglected and then put at such risk, with that most terrible of consequences in return.

But I acted as I did, and now I am here, in a wilderness that is entirely unexplored, and here and now, there is another state of being that is threatening to overcome me – for the first time in two millennia, I am afraid.

I am afraid of the vastness of the territory outside the Covenant.

And yet, and yet ...

As I look and see, as I tentatively sense and then explore, this wilderness is beautiful. It is vibrant, it is alive in a whole new way, in a different way.

It is violent, and it is powerful.

Most of all, it is calling to strands within me that I never even once suspected that they should be there at all – it is as though there is a part of me awakening from a long and frozen slumber, something raising, something rising, a power and an ancient strength, the very talents and abilities I need to not just enter into this new world outside the Covenant, but there to thrive, and to survive.

I stand of the threshold of my own becoming and I am in awe.

I am in awe of this new world, and I am in awe of me.

I turn to look upon myself and what I see is not what once I thought I knew.

It is entirely other than.

It is a being that I do not recognise, nor have the two millennia of existence leading up until this moment functioned to prepare me for this meeting.

I understand.

I understand that right here, right now, is the threshold to the next level.

I understand the Covenant, and I understand the choices that lie before me.

But what I don't yet know is how this understanding will be guiding all my actions and all the unfoldments that now rest upon the actions and decisions I will take within the next few moments, nor what result and repercussion will then follow in their trailing wakes.

Sadness

I take a moment to stabilise myself in timelessness, gather myself as if I was arranging a new cloak and straightening a crown upon my head that never have I known or worn before, yet all of that is me, the new me, the one I do not know as yet and who will only then unveil himself to me through my own deeds and actions.

Then I phase back into the streamings of unfoldment, subtly and gently, and so I am there exactly where I was when I first arrived, and the noise and repercussions on all the levels and the layers of my breach of the First Law are a veritable storm.

I stand cleanly in the center of the chaos of my own making and it enlivens me, delights me in a way that I could never have perceived or known before.

I raise a single hand and take command of the storm.

It comes to me, flows to me and finds an exit point in me; it flows into my structure and it is a union of a truly different kind and still, it is a union – the storm flows into me and in return, I give myself to where it once had been, and what I give is silence, safety, reflection, peace.

When the last of the storm has been consumed within me, I am entirely different yet again and the community is silent, reverent, white.

I adjust my perceptions and the four here in this room are also finally stilled to reverence and awe; all are on their knees, entirely tuned to me, wide open and yet, the pain of their transgressions is still with them, overwhelming, held at bay just for the moment by my actions and my choices.

I tune more closely to them and I feel a different rising; a soft yet cruel and shattering sensation and I know that I am sad.

"I am Gaius Decius Levinius, Segar Ta Cardor," I tell them so that their distinctive layers may begin to now align and come into a harmony that their existence needs so desperately at this time.

"I am here as part of my unfoldment and I am here to aid in yours."

There is a tremendous sense of relief and instant gratitude from the three young ones who as one, attempt to flow to me for safety and guidance. I hold them at bay and at a respectful distance, for I am not their Docem nor will I act in that capacity; that is not what is required here.

The fourth, the other, he is different.

I focus on him and to my surprise, I now no longer think of him as a monstrosity.

I understand!

He was born outside the Covenant, he is of that wild place where all that splendour and that fearful beauty lies and that is a part of me the same; and what I found so alien and so distasteful when first I touched the nature of his extraordinary being was exactly that – he is touched by the beautiful wild, is its child and in that way, not one of us.

We were all born to the Covenant and have to find our way through oh! so many different and gentle learnings and unfoldments to a place where we can even face the Wild without it tearing us apart – but he, he is born that way, for him, the Wild is father, mother and his Docem, too.

The concept renders me speechless.

The reality of the concept, a fully still material man who took the life of an Arada just like that, without the first of guidance, or instruction, simply because he could and it was there, is even more amazing still.

What should I say or do with one like that?

I cannot know that, and it is there, the Covenant returns to me.

When it does, such sadness falls upon me that I nearly swirl and lose cohesion – the Covenant is such a beautiful thing, such a wondrous thing, and it does not lose any of its glory or its power, within, or without.

There are undoubtedly unfoldments in the Beautiful Wild.

I cannot know what these might be, and it is quite enough that I should know there must be.

And more than that, there is the love.

It is a different love than I have come to know and understand, but love it is; and somewhere I suspect it is a greater kind of love in every way and so it is that I become aware that I was wrong – I am not outside the Covenant at all, but where I went is that I went outside of what I held the Covenant to be!

When I understand that, it is as though the world is coming back to me, and all and everything then falls into its rightful place, its rightful dance and all the sadness is now gone, and I can look upon the man with clarity and make my pledge that I should be his guardian and support him in his own unfoldments, wild, though they may be.

3: Markus Edwards, Docem

Angel

When the Segar Ta Cardor came to give us restitution and forbearance, I dissolved in gratitude and simply lay within myself, undone and helpless, and entirely at his mercy.

An angel he was, and as angel he did manifest; at first, I thought he was an angel of vengeance come to destroy us, delete us, wash away our sins and then, wash us away so that all of that had never been and no-one, no-one at all would so much as remember a whisper of our names.

It was excruciating pain, but I welcomed it, for I deserved that and so much more besides for my terrifying failure and the even more terrifying mistakes I had made. I welcomed his judgement hungrily and with desperation, for I could not be what I was and could find no way to absolve myself, dissolve myself, and not be there, responsible for it all.

But it was only for a moment that I thought that, that I had that hope of being alleviated in every way, of everything; the shining other stilled all to silence, and then I knew it would all go on, and there would be more, more unfoldments, more pain.

Possibly eternally.

But there was nothing I could do.

I was undone, and I was helpless, and I all I could do was watch as the Segar extended himself to reach and touch Burrows, my potential, my nemesis, the corner stone and catalyst of all this suffering and dissolution.

I wanted to cry out to the Segar, beg him not to hurt my potential, beg him to leave him be, to let him go and take me instead; I wanted to plead with him that the potential was in essence still an innocent, and no matter what he had done; that it wasn't his fault that he was left alone, without direction, without supervision and that he could not have known how to control a union, never even having had experience of one himself, not once.

I tried to rouse myself to intervene, but I was too weak and too dissolved, in far too many places all at once and I had no strength left, there was nothing I could do and I could not even turn away, not even phase away so I would not be here and have to know it all, and have to live these things.

I wish that I had still some eyes which could be closed; lids that would fall so gently over my burning eyeballs and bring with them, moisture and friendly dark, taking me away from this here and now; I wish I wasn't here alone, and even though I know it will not help me, I call for my Lady, call for Adela, and of course, she isn't there.

And then, there is nothing left for me to do but to submit.

Submit myself to here and now, and to accept what is to happen here in every way and let it be my punishment if it must be.

I actively then tune towards the Segar and the one I made and never even knew I did.

But what I see astonishes me.

The Segar takes a time to make exquisite fine adjustments and he phases into an existence that does resonate the states of being, alien and frightening as well they are, of my potential to a most profound degree.

I see him making a most subtle and most complex interlacement with Steve Burrows, that's his name, his designation is unknown; the Segar shows a range of deep vibrations I have never seen or yet experienced but they do resonate with Burrows, and it is done in deepest care and with a loving hand, and I fall away from that because I realise the Segar is acting in keeping with the Covenant.

He is treating Burrows with the same exquisite care of preciousness as would be given to the most beloved of Arada; the Segar is surrounding him, stabilising him, and communicating with him, and all without the slightest hint of union, either way.

I feel a further shame descend then upon me and make me even weaker still; how could I have lost trust in our Covenant?

Here it is, here it is, alive and in action.

The Segar is loving my potential, and in so doing, he is healing him, forgiving him, and saving him and his unfoldments absolutely.

114

Assistance

When I become conscious again, and manifest again to know and think and to remember, the world is a different place.

Time has not shifted significantly; all the material components are still in place very much the way they were after I had first awoken to the screams of the Arada as a one of their gentle circle fell away, and failed to be, and altogether left the realms of our existence.

When I had rushed into the Underworld and found my own potential lying face down in a pile of glittering ashes that once had been Xiao Hong, and I failed to recognise him for he was so thoroughly changed by having taken a late stage Arada and made her his own in one fell rushing and without returning the exchange.

When all the wailing all around me had begun to crest and crest, higher and higher, further and wider as the community cried out in pain across the times and spaces of unfoldment, and when my Cestra clung to me and screeched into my ears and tore at me, ripped me into pieces and all I knew that it had all been of my doing, everything was my fault.

When I took Burrows away from what I could not be in the presence of and all of us had hidden in my room and tried to shield ourselves from the accusations and the horror of the situation.

I remember it all, and none of it destabilises me now to any great extend.

The Segar has healed me, and his work has been exquisite.

I am calm, and perfectly aware of everyone, and everything.

I kneeling on the floor in my rooms in what had been my Lady Adela's house. On my left side is Alexandra, and she too is still and receptive. Beside her kneels Satari, open and ready. On my right, I feel and see Burrows, my potential, ah ...

He is kneeling just the same as we are, directed forward and to the Segar, who stands before us and now appears as a great man of middle age, strong built, with iron grey hair and bright eyes, wearing a dark blue suit of exquisite cut and material.

I understand that the Segar's appearance is a fine creation that has strands of truth most elegantly interlaced with subtle small adjustments, specially created for Steve Burrows, so that he sees and feels a something here that will make sense and speak to him correctly, and directly, in a way that he can understand.

Burrows is a bright flame of many colours.

I have never seen anything like that.

There is rushing inside of him, a powerful upward draft that is connected not in a communal way but to the very Earth itself? Or to another source of energy? It is confusing, new, different, but then there is also a resonance there – I think, yes, I believe that I saw that in him when first we met. It was deep underground, but the shadow of it ...

This is the same structure, only the form is more evolved.

Whatever Burrows is, he is evolving.

He is unfolding.

It is fascinating and I am beginning to wonder if ...

The Segar addresses us all, calmly, and at the multi-level, so that all four of us experience a sense that he is speaking exactly to each one, and them alone, so perfect is his alignment in four very different dimensions, all at the same time.

He speaks of times and unfoldments, of certain points where the old folds into the new; where there seems to be uncontrolled chaos but it is only thus because we don't know or recognise these unfoldments.

I nod as he speaks and transmits these knowings, and these truths.

The others do the same.

The Segar tells us that he is not here to be our Docem; that he cannot guide our various unfoldments, but that he is offering his assistance, what wisdom and strength he has to aid us at this time where all is new and no-one knows what happens next.

We instinctively and as one, breathe a sigh of gratitude and of devotion; this makes me aware that the Segar is bonding us, weaving us together, restoring the bonds that must have been damaged or broken completely when all these things had come to pass, and every one of us changed rapidly, in many different directions, like frightened birds will scatter when a hawk appears within their midst.

I admire the Segar's work; I can't conceive of what it takes to do what he is doing here and now, with such precision and exactitude; so gently and unnoticeably; and though I try and track exactly what it is he is doing, so I might learn from this, I soon become aware that what I notice is less than the smallest tip of an island that reaches far under the sea, far, further than the highest mountain.

I breathe out a mist and let it go then; I am no longer sure of my unfoldments but should the Universe decree that it should happen, the day will come and I will be a Segar, I will know what this is from the other side, and from my deepest wells there rises then the pledge and the desire that I should be as pure and radiant and have the Covenant around my shoulders like a royal cloak in that most intimate way this Segar has it with him, a part of him, and this is what is making him so much, and so much more than any of us are or dream that we could be.

The Segar looks to me and he smiles; it is a touch of resonance that has the scent of morning mists and first and gentle rays of sunlight over forests, old and deep and it gladdens me, it honours me.

A fleeting whisper, intimate and heard by me alone, informs me that I should be steady as my time would come; he will address now one by one, each one of us and help us lay a pathway that will take us out of this and straight into the new, whatever it may be.

I bow my head to him, I bow my own self to him in deep respect and deference, and thus he turns and asks Satari to come forward, and to join him in a private consultation to determine what her path should be.

Satari looks to me, and I am surprised, amused and a little pleased that even after all that we'd been through, she would still honour me, her Docem. Her small act of respect touches me, and it heals a place that had been left by the Segar's intervention; it might be that it was a something he had not within his power to bestow, and that it was Satari's own to give to me.

I love her with all my heart, and bless her; she rises, and goes to the Segar without hesitation. He enfolds her in a gentle sphere of safety and intimacy and both phase from this time and place.

Ghosts & Galaxies

The room, the house and all beyond is quiet.

I am clear and lightly balanced; the absence of the Segar has released me in a way and so I rise and flex myself.

Steve looks up at me, and his bearing is such that I stop.

For all the Segar's interventions, he is still intensely aware of his great crime and carries it as a burden; for all the Segar's interventions, he is still intensely uncomfortable in this new that has befallen him.

I understand that I alone is now what makes the bridge for him between the then, and now, and that it is me he needs, no matter that I lack the knowledge, power and accomplishments.

I nod for I understand this. When Satari acknowledged me, and in so doing, gave me back my rank of Docem in that instance, it was her action that was needed to make the change for me; no Segar, nor an Essem could have done this for me – but my Cestra sister could.

So I accept this as a fact and hold out my hand to Burrows, fully manifest and physical in every way.

He takes it hesitantly, and I grasp his hand strongly and pull him to his feet.

For an instant, he is surprised at my strength, then a tired shadow of a smile washes over him and he nods his thanks.

He takes a moment to balance himself as well, then he runs his hand through his hair and asks me, "And what now? What's going to happen to me? To you?"

I find it difficult to keep my focus on him as a man, for I can see and feel the fire inside of him, and it is drawing my fascination. With a will, I tune away from that and answer him at his own level, "The Segar told me he will speak with each of us in turn, to help us come to a decision as regards our respective futures."

"Does that include me?" asks Burrows.

I nod re-assurance. "Yes, of course it does," and when that isn't still quite getting through, I add carefully, "After all, you are still my potential."

Burrows shakes his head and against his will, starts to laugh, a racking, sore laugh that seeks to turn itself into something else, into an outburst of sorrow, but he battles it, forces himself to cough instead.

Alexandra moves to him and steps close, then places an arm around his waist; he hesitates, turns to her and she embraces him fully.

"It's alright," she whispers and her whisper echoes down into the other levels, soothing his disturbances, "It wasn't your fault. It was mine."

It takes me a moment to realise that she isn't just saying that in order to stabilise Steve Burrows, but that there is the weight of burden behind that statement that tells me that she believes this to be true.

Burrows straightens from the embrace, tries to step back but Alexandra won't let him go. He is shaking his head. "No," he says, "It isn't your fault! How can you say that! It was me who ..."

I step forward swiftly and with force.

"Both of you, be silent," I command them and that is the first time I have used the power of the Docem to be heard and there be no denying my voice. Burrows and my Cestra freeze in position, then turn to me as one.

"I am your Docem. Are you willing to challenge me for the responsibility over these events?" I ask them clearly and with force.

Alexandra immediately drops her eyes, lets go of Burrows and bows to me deeply.

"No, my Lord Markus," she whispers.

Burrows struggles but he holds my eyes and we do battle in the strangest way, on the strangest level – it is a most peculiar form of union, one of rejection rather than infusion, but a form of union it is, and it is quite enjoyable. We to and fro quite playfully for a time, and finally, Burrows smiles and bows his head and says, "No, my Lord Markus," but there is no submission whatsoever in that statement, and he has reserved his right to retain his own guilt and responsibility for the events.

Still, I am satisfied. I see no problem with him doing that; just as long as he doesn't take on more than belongs to him by rights, all should be well and the burdens balanced as they should, and easier to bear.

I feel the need to get it all out now, to get a movement and I breach the subject and say, "Xiao Hong has gone. This is the reality. We all feel her loss most keenly, and the empty place she leaves in our futures. Each one of us has, in their own way, contributed to these events and that cannot be denied. But I am Docem, and it was in me she placed her trust when she became Arada – not in me as who I am, please understand, but in the institution. I am Docem, and it was my first commandment above all else to protect the Arada, for they cannot protect themselves and place their lives into my hands. Whatever either of you did, or did not do, and yes, that includes you, Steve, it does not compare with my failure to protect Xiao Hong. I would have that be understood by both of you."

Alexandra is open and full of sadness at the remembrance of the beautiful Arada she had tended for all her Cestra life, and who was so much a part of her, and even more so for the smallness and the intimacy of our house as was. She bows in response to my words and says, "I will always carry her with me."

Steve Burrows swallows hard and then he says, "I do carry her with me. I really do ..." and then he puts his hands before his face, steps back and lets himself slide to the ground, dissolved in sadness and guilt and something else that I can't track or trace.

I stare at him and I begin to wonder what it might be like, what it would feel like, to take another's life in all totality and until there was absolutely nothing left of them.

I can't begin to imagine. I am afraid to begin to imagine.

I ask him, "What was it like? How did it feel when you ... took her?"

Burrows shakes his head, still in his hands, and then he looks up at me. He looks exhausted, his body is exhausted even though the fire within is burning as bright as ever, possibly even brighter still.

"Do you not know?" he asks hoarsely.

Alexandra goes and sits beside him on the floor. Gently, she tells him, "When we do this – we call it the union – we take very carefully, and we give back from within ourselves in exchange, so that a balance is kept. It takes a long time to learn how to do that."

I recognise her words and her demeanour. She is speaking as she would, and she has, to any new potential, to any one who didn't know about our lives, the Covenant and how we move through our unfoldments with exquisite elegance and grace. It strikes me strangely that I should have never told Steve Burrows all these things, these basic things, nor that I felt he needed to hear them.

I might have been confused or mistaken, for Steve turns to Alexandra with attention and with gratitude for the information. He says, "That makes sense. And I guess it explains why it takes so long to make the transformation. Centuries, he told me."

Alexandra nods. "Sometimes, it really does take that long. Not always though. Half a century is about average, but it depends on the circumstances and everyone involved."

Burrows sighs. "And I took all of her in – a moment, in one night?"

Alexandra and I are both too stunned by the actuality of this, the reality of this, and the fact that we had never even thought to do a thing like he had done, nor heard of it, in all our times, in all of our instructions and so we don't respond.

Burrows asks uncertainly, "So does that make me one of you now?"

I and my Cestra exchange a brief contact and I respond with care, "Not quite yet. There is still the choosing, and the festival."

This isn't strictly true, however. Steve Burrows will never be one of us. Not ever. To be one of us as he has termed it, the transformation would have needed to proceed in care and gentle, fine unfoldments.

I have no idea what he is now, but he isn't one of us. He is something else and he will never find an entrance as Arada in a house, nor spend his time of dreaming gently, and of learning our ways. And thus, he can't be Cestra, and he can't be Docem after that, and then Ferata, Segar, Cardor, Essem ... all of these futures do not exist for him, not in the way we know them.

This troubles me deeply until I remember what the Segar had told me – he would give his insights and his wisdom to the situation, and he would help me come to a decision, the same as he would help Steve Burrows and my Cestra Alexandra too.

"When is the festival?" asks Burrows, "How much time has passed? What is the day? What is the time?"

I can tell him at least this much with certainty. "Today is Saturday. It is around midnight and we'll be entering Sunday soon, so there are three days left to the festival."

"I haven't eaten anything since this afternoon," says Burrows and for a moment I am appalled and think he means what happened in the Underworld, then I remember that he is still entirely corporeal and that his body has a variety of needs that cannot yet be stilled with the Water Of Life alone.

Alexandra and I step into a rapid exchange that is out of his range as yet, at least the details of the communication pass him by even if he knows it is occurring for he can sense this. He is very aware, very aware indeed.

Alexandra touches him on the arm and smiles at him. "I will get you something to eat," she says, "Is there anything special you would like?"

Burrows half smiles, half grimaces, shakes his head, then tells her, "I don't care, as long as it comes with black coffee and sugar. And whiskey. Yeah, I need a drink."

She smiles and nods, then she gets up and is halfway to the door when she turns back, suddenly uncertain again.

"May I leave?" she asks outright, and I know she is worried about the Segar. I send her re-assurance and ask her for good speed, and she rushes off so fast, she goes straight through the door without stopping to open it first.

"Whoa," says Burrows, "Man! I don't think I'll ever get used to that ..." and then, silence descends on the room.

I go to my bed and sit down on it, then lie down. Then I release the burden of this tight manifestation to physicality and phase into a more comfortable state, which involves becoming see-through and floating a little way above the physical surface of the bed.

I emanate a sense of relief at this state, and Burrows picks it up.

From where he is on the other side of the room, he says, "You look like a ghost. Does it feel – nice? To be like that?"

Not having a body and being unwilling to go through the trouble of shaping and creating resonances that would produce physical sound, I reach out to him, mesh with him lightly and transmit the experience of my state directly instead.

He enjoys this, but the meshing counter-transference gives me a better indication of just how tired he is, how hungry he is, how stressed and how his body is in pain of tension all over. These sensations make me shudder. It has been a long time since I remember feeling likewise, all the time, and now I am no longer used to such extreme levels of discomfort, everywhere, and all the time.

I have quite forgotten how hard it used to be ...

Burrows speaks into my thoughts. "I snuck into your room when you were sleeping," he says slowly and quietly. "I saw you. You were a galaxy ..." and through his eyes, I see myself, the way a human would perceive, and feel his wonder, and his longing.

I have never seen myself that way.

"Come here," I send him and he rises, walks across to the bed, hesitates briefly, then lies down carefully without touching my misty shape. That is what he sees, but of course, what I am is spread out far and wide; even on the other side of the room, he is already inside of me, if only he knew that.

Perhaps he did.

I extinguish the light in the room, then shift across further, and further still, until I rise cleanly and find the threshold of the state of dreaming, but I don't enter all the way. Burrows looks up at me, and all his tiredness and pain is now forgotten; entirely fascinated, he is watching me, and tracing my unfoldments, minute sparks of everlasting evolution, and at last, he is at peace.

Inferno

From my half dream position on the ceiling, perceiving down of course I sense and now experience the strange conversion, half man and half unknowable existence in a new way and from a different vantage point.

He had described me as a galaxy, and there are aspects of that in his system too; there are swirls and interlacements, sparkling river streams that might evoke such an idea, such a description.

But that is strictly peripheral to the symphony of fire in his center; what I had perceived to be a column is a disk that spins and that extends in all directions, creating an updraft in its center where it spins fast, very fast indeed; that is the rushing that I felt inside of him.

The colours are intense; there are so many strands, so many interlacements but themselves, the colour streams are pure as pure can be, and they are dense, much denser than I've ever seen or known, much denser than any kind of colour stream or incidence I can remember even from Adela – the only time I've felt something remotely like this was inside the Segar, but even there, it was not nearly as profound and powerful as this.

I am drawn to the spiralling fire colours and as I begin to feel a fascination coming to me, and a wish to taste them, touch them so I could learn of their existence, make them a part of me I become aware that these colours in turn are seeking me, that they are under pressure, and that their flow will be a charge, a furious, roaring inferno should I make just the smallest breach or even an attempt at a connection.

I hold back then and fight my fascination, fight my hunger for these colours, try to reverse my forward movement but it is already way too late – the colours have existence of their own, they have awareness that I'm here and I cannot now escape – they rise up, all at once, a rainbow curtain of such density and splendour that I lose all sense of this or that.

I accept the reality. I accept the challenge.

I let go and I swoop into a forward dive, into submission, into union –
here I come, here it is, so let it be.

4: Designation Unknown

Union

I lay on Edward's bed and stared up at the galaxy that slowly spun directly above me and I forgot everything for a moment.

Ah, the relief.

I wanted to just sink into this sensation of finally being somewhere safe, somewhere calm and beautiful and dissolve myself to the experience of the galaxy but my eyes were grainy, hot and dry and I kept wanting to close them.

But I did not want to close my eyes for then I would no longer see this miracle he had created in response to what I told him and how I felt about that; so I fought and struggled and this came between me and the moment, ever worse until at last, I gave up and I closed my eyes.

It was extraordinary.

Not only could I still clearly see the galaxy above, I saw it far more clearly, saw it in its real reality, not confined by ceilings, bedposts, ordinariness – now, it was no longer an alien intrusion into an establish world, but it was right at home, and oh, it was so beautiful!

He was so beautiful!

So distant and so cool, so endless, so restful, so complete and so – incredibly attractive to me, so homeward calling, if I could go there, be there, reach into the center then I too could be still. The cool and calm and the vastness of that space would take that pressure out of me, would let me give it up and become free of it, become free of that alien presence I had taken, made my own and which now ruled me with its unimaginable demands, sensations.

I saw the galaxy and I prayed to it, I prayed that I would be allowed to go and be there, come home, be saved, be relieved and then I could feel it opening up to me, it wanted me the same to bring this fire and to warm its very core.

Permission was all that I had needed and so I flooded towards that silent space, I burst my dams and roared upward, forward and out, became an ocean wave of light and for a moment I could feel a hesitation, or a fear and yet it lasted only for the fraction of a heartbeat, then there was a welcome and entire wide embrace as what I was and what it was collided – it was no shock, there was no reverberation or percussion, and when we touched and then began to flow into each other, it was as though what I was and what he was were exactly made to be the perfect match, the perfect answer to each other's questions, the solution to the limitations of each other's states of being.

I gave fire and in return, I harvested the brilliant ice of stars and darkness in a tapestry that made them one and all the same, and as we rippled, as we spread, and as we fed upon each other, giving and receiving in return, I could perceive a threshold coming closer, coming closer – and beyond that threshold lay salvation, there lay treasure of a kind I never knew to ask for or to hope, expect; there lay reward and rescue all the same, and then I knew that this was transformation.

White Space

All around me, everything is white.

This white is made up of a myriad of lights so infinitely small that they are dense and everywhere at once, and it glows from its own existence, within and without.

I am here, and I am thinking.

I am me, Steve Burrows is my name, and I am sensing, feeling, seeing and experiencing here in this white space that is only one way, and that is holy.

I know he is here and I call to him, the best I can – he hears me instantly and now, I am not sure if there is any distance left between us, or if I am mistaken and we are just one, not two.

"Edwards? Where are we?"

Before the thought is finished I already know that he has no idea and is as new to this, as newly born to this as I am, and he knows I know and therefore gives me no response.

"What happened? Who are we?"

That is the same again and for some reason, this amuses me; it amuses him too and once again I get this feeling that this space we share might just be more than just ...

"We completed the union."

Did I think that, or did he?

Does it matter?

We completed the union. Indeed, we did. We went across a threshold and it changed us into something altogether new.

"What now?"

Who thought that? I don't know. I try and turn around somehow to face him, but it feels like only one turning, only a single movement in this space. The movement leaves behind itself a starry trail of brighter light and it fascinates me.

It fascinates me ...

I have a recollection of the colours I first saw in what they call the Underworld, and then another joins it – it is a recollection of the colours once again, but I have never seen this? Whose are they, what is this?

It is I, and I remember seeing me from Edward's vantage, and in some loss of understanding I attempt to move from one of these and to the other, to know just what is what and whose is which, but they are the same.

Are we the same?

"Edwards, what has happened here?"

But this time, there is only the resonance of my own thoughts, a vague echo, nothing more and I begin to be afraid.

Have I murdered him too?

Have I murdered – me?

The white is all around.

It is alive, singing and dancing with aliveness.

I am not alone and even though I cannot now perceive another like myself, I am comforted.

We are comforted.

We are in the light.

The light.

PART 3

1: Alexandra Zyskowska

White Light

I evoked riversmooth before picking up the telephone and dialling the only number I knew, that of our house Assay, John Eldrich 3rd.

"This is Adela Bach," I told the answer machine and the line immediately switched and only seconds later, I heard Mr Eldrich, his voice hoarse but his mind most instantly awoken by my use of the password that identified me as being one of this house.

"How can I serve you, Madam?" he enquired most politely.

"I need a selection of food delivered immediately," I tell him, "It is to include fresh black coffee and whiskey."

There is a momentary silence, then Eldrich asks carefully, "To serve how many? And should this be a dinner or buffet food?"

I can't think about these things, I can't be going to that far into a past to even begin to engage in this conversation. "Bring a selection, enough for three ..." and I swallowed the word "humans" from the end of the sentence as that would have been in breach of the very strict regulations that pertained to telephone conversations with the house Assay in the middle of the night.

"Bring it as soon as possible and with all speed," I tell him and can feel that he bowing, even though he is at the end of a telephone as he says, "Yes, of course, Madam. Right away."

I put the telephone down and considered that strictly speaking, this was no longer Adela Bach's house and therefore, Eldrich was not the assigned Assay any longer either. No transference ritual had taken place on Lady Adela's leaving – just another minor infraction, irregularity to add to all the major ones.

I am sure the Segar and Lord Markus will sort it all out, and all will be well.

With all speed, I return to Lord Markus' room but as I am about to enter, I become aware of a very strange energy inside, emanating from the room.

It is very strange indeed, and it is disturbing. It makes me shiver, it makes me insecure and at the same time, it is fascinatingly attractive – I carefully phase through the door but remain unmanifest so I can observe without causing a disturbance.

Something very strange is happening here.

I seen Lord Markus near to dreaming above the bed, and on the bed lies the human, or half human, or whatever he is, Burrows, and there are colours rising from him, strong colours, curtains of colours rising up towards my Lord, who so it seems in turn is folding in and around and stretching towards the colours at the same time – I freeze inside and out as I understand that I am in the presence of a union!

I should not be here, should not witness this, for this is a most private moment, yet I am too fascinated and appalled, I cannot move, I cannot leave and furthermore, I'm being drawn to this which is a fascinating spectacle on every level and in every way.

There is a wave of resonance arising even though there is such an inordinate difference between the two who are attempting a connection and a union here; it is as though two opposites have found each other, two things that can be neither here nor there, and they are getting closer and they touch – I fear the worst but what happens next is quite impossible for me to talk about or even understand.

Where there were two approaching systems, in an instant they implode into each other in a starbust flare of purest white that blinds me on all levels, wipes out every sense of any kind and yet it isn't painful or explosive, but liquid – that is all I can say, the movement is liquid, liquid living light of transformation and I am left with that brightwhite sensation for a time unknowable, before slowly, slowly, my receivers come back on line, feedback from the environment, from myself, slowly I can sense again, straining through mist and resonance of whiteness, and until it does recede, becomes fainter, I can see again, and I can hear, and I can know the Segar has returned, called to this extraordinary union of unfoldment, and I can see just one, a single system flowing liquid white and light between the space that once had been Steve Burrows, and Lord Markus.

Beautiful

I look to the Segar for help and draw to him more closely, step more closely into his field of strength and power and try to see through his eyes, try to understand what happened here, what or who that is now, because I don't know, I've never seen or heard of such a thing.

The Segar is riveted, absolutely fascinated; I can feel wavelike motions phasing in and out as he tracking levels and layers which I don't understand, to which I have no access; but he isn't understanding this either, and his sense of surprise, awe and wonderment does not alleviate in any way.

Far away, like hushing, rushing whisper I can sense the community; they too all know that something has happened but no-one knows what it is. I tune closer to the Segar still and am comforted that he is not disturbed or fearful; he is just observing so it might not be yet another disaster, yet another disturbance, yet another thing forbidden and to fill me with more shame and terror still.

The Segar has become aware of me and he steps back so that he can be focussed both on me and on that alien creation still hovering in purest opalescence just above the bed; it shifts in shape in smooth and liquid motions, ripples like slow mist now and then.

It is very beautiful.

I can sense the Segar speaking to me, to himself and all who might be listening, "You are right, young Cestra. It is beautiful indeed."

"What is it?" I ask as I am more and more drawn to this ... being? existence? unfoldment?

I can feel the Segar smile as he responds most kindly, "It is precious."

I look to the white and radiant existence and I must agree. Yes, it is precious. It is also unfolding, it is in evolution.

But is it loved?

The Segar turns to me in preference, and his most powerful existence takes my attention away from the being of white and focuses me entirely on him instead.

"Is it loved?" he asks me and his voice and meanings resonate throughout my structure, make me vibrate, fine and finer still until like mist the fear, uncertainty and all things past arise and disappear and leave me clear and bright as a landscape in the morning sunshine.

There, I can see, and I can see far and wide.

And there, I know the only answer can be, "Yes. Oh yes, it is beloved."

"It is of the Covenant," the Segar says and even though I am not sure precisely what he means by that, or could explain it, was I asked, I know deep down in every fibre of my structure that he is right, and more than that – it may not be just of the Covenant, but in the strangest sense, I feel this being is the Covenant itself – manifest, and come to us, as it was promised long ago.

The Segar stills as my idea, my intuition strikes him straight and true right at his center; then he expands and comes to me, comes closer and closer still and offers me a union.

I am spun in all directions; I am overwhelmed and gratified; terrified and honoured; and with a breathless grace I rise to him, I bow to him and offer all I am to him.

He picks me up and raises me, raises me higher and higher, far above and beyond any place I have ever been, up and up, higher and brighter, and with every rising so expands my freedom, expands my power and expands my choice to see him more and more, to now be able to perceive just where I need to touch him, want to touch him, want to give to him and take from him in equal measure.

It is exquisite and unlike any union I have ever known; it is fantastic, sky blue, rose hues, opalescent purples intertwining richest emerald greens and azure, colours like I've never seen and songs, and sounds I've never heard – are they mine, are they his, it matters not, they flow and we are one in dance, in joy, in ecstasy.

Treasures

Gaius is lovingly surrounding me when I awaken to him, holding me gently and loving me most deeply at the same time.

I know his times, I know his spaces; I know him intimately and thus I know that he held nothing back, and gave me everything he was, everything he had to give and oh! what treasures did he give me!

How did he change me!

How did he awaken me!

My gratitude is such that is breezes through him like a fair storm, sweeping from the mountains and into the valleys, telling of heights above and far vistas, gladly enfolded, and hope, and the first fine grass of spring.

I feel as though it wasn't until now that I was truly chosen, that my transformation had truly become complete, or that I truly understand our kind, or our relationships.

Of course, I think that is because I am so young but Gaius sends me a negation and he tells me that it is the same for him, that all and any time and any union never did compare to what had happened there between us, in the presence of ...

Instantly, we manifest more tightly and begin to think now in a different way. We are still deeply bonded and one thought will travel through us both; this causes us to resonate in joy once more as patterns and appearances, cause and effect, the future and the past become so clearly now defined and interlaced, and we can read it all, and easily.

The white being, it caused this.

It catalysed us.

Being in its presence, we undertook a union in a different way; there was no thought of levels, of propriety; there was no care or cautious holding back the flow for fear of losing far too much or being burned or doing wrong – it was a union that was natural and as it always should have been between two of our kind ... and more.

And more?

I try to track that fascinating thought but it disappears swiftly and there is too much of Gaius that is too delicious and to wondrous still; I snuggle to him and let him stroke me, let him celebrate me, me, Alexandra, no longer Cestra, no longer anything, just me, and I am ...

"Gaius, what are we?" I ask him in all sincerity, for I no longer feel that I am comfortable with the designation of what I used to think was "my kind".

Gaius doesn't answer because he doesn't know; but he agrees with me that we are no longer that, but other than.

We are other than other than.

It is an unfoldment. It is absolutely derived from love. And it is precious.

We smile in harmony for we both know that not only did the Covenant allow for the coming of our kind, it predicted it inside its very structure.

There is a transformation beyond the transformation – who ever was to know?

Who ever was to guess?

"The Cardor know," he tells me and directs my attention to the place within himself that holds that information and I let that stream to me, a delightful union in and of itself, satisfying, tingling, it makes me giggle.

"Ah! But if you think my love, such little things, and how joyous they are, and how many of our kind live for eternities and never feel this pleasure?"

"It has been written and foretold that one would come who would be our saviour, who would set us free."

There is no doubt in either of our minds on any level that the one did come.

They did not come from far away, but they arose by union right from those we knew amongst our midst – who would ever have guessed?

For all these unknown time spans we had searched and waited for a special potential who alone would be the one.

It is understandable how such a mistake might have been made.

But was it a mistake?

I am wondering ...

Gaius tells me lovingly, "We should return to our unfoldments, many layers, many levels, and there is the physical as well. There are unfoldments there just the same, and important they are, even if they seem mundane."

I agree with him.

So on many levels, we remain interwoven and in a standing, radiant harmony of union that hasn't ended just because we became aware of who we are once more; and on some other levels, we regain our material manifestations of choice, and re-enter what the humans call reality.

Service

Gaius and I are standing at the foot of what used to be my brother's bed, and then my Docem's.

I try to get a sense of mourning or of loss but it is hard to do; I feel as though what once was Mark is still here, that it isn't gone at all and even that I might converse, communicate with that essential center that is so uniquely he once more.

The beautiful and unknown alien entity is shimmering and touching all the room, the house and surroundings with its radiance.

Gaius says very softly, "It is new. It is becoming."

I am in agreement. It has a feeling of Arada in a way, a dreamy drifting that is necessary to conserve energy as one thing turns into another, a metamorphosis unfoldment, a very magical thing indeed.

"Do we need to guard it?" I ask him just as softly for I would not wish to disturb the entity or distract it from its proper course.

Gaius sends me a half balanced negation and unknowingness; I think we both feel strongly that this entity does not need our protection, and yet we feel a sense of caretaking towards it, a parental responsibility of sorts.

The entity and each other is absorbing us altogether, and it is not until we notice a shift in the entity's existence that we too become aware of a disturbance not too far away.

Both Gaius and I immediately sweep across and down to where the center of events that have disturbed our entity is located; and I feel a moment's brushing guilt sensation when I realise it is the human Assay I had called I don't know when or just how long ago.

He has been standing outside our door for a long time.

The man is in a high state of disturbance; he is suffering from numerous physical symptoms and is near to collapse.

Action needs to be taken, and immediately so.

Gaius and I both manifest ourselves just inside the second door, take on a suitable shape and I open the doors physically to find old Mr

Eldrich, half doubled over, shaking with cold, behind a pile of boxes in the pouring rain.

My heart goes out to him in every way.

It literally goes out to him, and wraps him in a warming cocoon, I draw him inside towards me and then physically place my arm about his shoulders – he is shaking hard and is finding it hard to breathe.

I bring him inside and Gaius physically collects the boxes, drenched wet they are and some have collapsed into themselves, and I take Mr Eldrich to the drawing room, sit him down on the sofa.

This is not enough.

This old man came when I called him in the depth of night, for no reward other than to serve what used to be my kind.

True, his payment was received upfront – once he had been a potential, and had been given the conversion gift as is the law. But that was long ago; indeed, so long ago, that he and I might have been at the self same festival and I was chosen, when he was not.

Time, Restored

He is old, he is tired, he is cold and he is in bitter pain.

There is a resonance of warnings, of forbidden things, but that is just a shadow.

In my mind, there is the entity upstairs, and there is Gaius and our union, and the new of all of that; and so I reach inside myself and offer the old man a union – I will take your pain, your cold and all your burdens, and in return, I'll give you of my fire, warmth and love.

His lack of strength is such that he but crawls toward me; so I don't even wait to meet him halfway but instead, I bring myself to him and gently make the first connections, and I let his suffering come to me, and invite it in, I draw it to me and I drink it, bitter wine, old wine, old times, all the times remembered; it does not hurt me and it is just as it is, and carefully I then begin to feed him me, the new me, the shinier, stronger me, the other me and here it is delightful to see him grow to that, and grow with that, and change with that as well.

This union has a natural conclusion.

When his tastes and textures become smooth and free in flow, light and easy, and relieved of all the staleness and the old, I gently disengage from him and just before I let the last of the direct connections go, I use it to transmit a loving, an acknowledgement and a gratitude for all his years of service.

On the couch before me, the old man whose hands I hold in mine is still wet through and through, and he is still old; but he is clear and smiling, he is present and he is in love.

Gaius directs me discreetly to tune to the entity above to notice what my actions had achieved, and it is most delightful to feel it being happy too, it has receded to its previous state and it is satisfied.

The old man shivers again and draws my attention; I have restored his systems at that level but he can still quite easily get unfortunate repercussions from his physical states.

"It would be best if you took off your wet clothes and rested in one of the rooms tonight," I say to him and listen with some wonder to the echoes of a voice that seems not mine, it is gentle and different, or perhaps I just experience it differently now.

"Your clothes can dry while you – sleep."

The old man looks up and around the room in shock, then at me and asks curiously, "Are you sure? Are you sure this would be acceptable?"

"I am sure," I say and smile, hold out my hand and he takes it immediately.

I lead him upstairs and find him an empty bedroom on the second floor. He is amazed that the stairs hold no challenge and he can walk and breathe so easily. He wants to thank me, but I send him a knowing that there is no need for that, which widens his pale eyes and he falls silent.

Before I leave him in the room, I tell him that when he awakes he should leave right away and without delay; he promises me fervently that he will do as I asked and so I bid him a good night.

Gaius appears at my shoulder outside the human's room.

He is curious to know more about the union I had made with the human; and he wonders if there will be any side effects.

The only unions between humans and our kind that we're familiar with is the first union, when a potential becomes Arada; after that, we have no congress with these others any longer.

I remember that I questioned the validity of that the night I sat with Burrows and I watched him breathe, and dream, and move and turn in his sleep, and all his many emanations.

Together, we tune to the old man who is stripping off his clinging garments, wrapping himself into a bed sheet and looking around in wonder.

The union has left a resonant connection that through me, Gaius is sharing. We are fascinated by this close contact, this insight into another, and it is another, not just one of them, far away and immaterial, a single beast from a herd of billions – this old man is one, and he has unfoldments; he is loved, and he is precious.

Gaius and I breathe a sigh of sorrow that we should have so long failed to realise the truth of that, how we walked in blindness, more so for him who walked for so much longer than I ever did.

The old man is thinking of the past.

He is remembering his festival.

His recollections are so clear, so vibrant and so intense, it shudders us both through and through and it brings to us the reality of our own festivals, and the fact that we were absolutely once what he has been, we were the same – how could we have forgotten?

How could we have forgotten stepping down and down, down and down the beautifully laid out, enormous stairwell that is a well indeed, and we are going to its center, deep down into the Earth. Many others step down with us, and we are all entranced; we are all afraid; we all vibrating with our own hopes and passions.

The stairs seem to go on forever, impossibly endless long and deep and finally, there is the emergence through a great vaulted arc of shining gold into the theatre, and that is too much to take in all at once, and here, the images become flashes, unconnected scenes of the high vaulted stands all around, the sensations of presence, faces at the balconies, you must keep moving, you are caught in a stream of others like you, you are a part of a river stream that flows towards the sea, the central space; and then, there is the music, felt not heard at first, and I saw musicians playing alien instruments on a low stage, impossible waterfalls of velvet curtains behind them, and the music began to take me over, take me away, make me sway and turn me inside out, it makes me feel like singing, singing the song of my heart, of my soul for this is my music, come to give me wings this night, allow me to release all shields and all illusions and be here, just myself, be me, sing me, call out, call for the one ...

And here, the path of our shared recollections divides and thus, I come back to myself and our close and triple union, Cestra, Segar and human has unwoven but it was, undoubtedly it was.

Gaius and I are too overwhelmed to communicate at first, but soon enough we stabilise and then we understand that we had taken back our human lives, we had bridged back and through, and now, our time was healed.

The great divide had been broken.
The truth is this.
We are one, and the same.

2: John Eldrich 3rd, House Assay

Awakenings

I awoke in the house of Adela Bach, sitting wrapped in a linen bed sheet on a great four poster bed.

I did not awake from sleep, or from a dream; I awoke from my life.

With extraordinary clarity I understood that I had become ensnared in a fantasy, no, not a fantasy, a moment in time; and I had lived there and not here, for all this time.

There was a stillness in me that I don't recall ever having felt before.

I could understand cause and effect, I knew that I had sacrificed my entire life for that single moment when first I met the beautiful Lady who held out the promise to me that I could immortal and perhaps, her lover.

I can see her face, her smile as clearly as though she was right here in the room with me; yet it was sixty years ago that last I saw her.

Sixty years.

I was inside of that for all those years, encapsulated; trapped; and it was all there was for me.

I never knew that I was a prisoner.

I never knew.

My breathing is rich and deep, such as it has not been for many years now; the Lady downstairs healed me in a wondrous way, and she healed more than just my cold, my pain, my failing breath and my struggling heart.

She set me free.

Now, I am outside of the prison I entered so gladly and so willingly and I see me, across the time of my life, clinging to every and any keepsake, souvenir that bound me to them, to her – utility bills that had to be paid, repairs that had to be overseen; sometimes and rarely, travel arrangements.

Each and every one was a holy service to me, and I would so lovingly tend to each and every one with the furious devotion of a virgin priest tending the flames on his altar.

My gods were just as elusive as his.

Now, here, and from the outside, I can see clearly that they never talked to me unless they absolutely had to; that they wanted no part of me beyond having someone to deal with those things that did not concern them, but which existed nonetheless and without which they would have to live in fields and meadows.

But then, and on the inside, it wasn't like that.

I was permanently in love, lived in permanent faith and trust that today might be the day, the day was here when the phone would ring, a messenger would come, I would be called somewhere, and there she would be, welcoming me, taking me in her arms, and the waiting would be over.

Oh, I did not suffer!

No man did more gladly reject the offers of human companionship, of fellowship or romance than I!

I had only one love, my service, and nobody and nothing was ever allowed to come between me and my altar, my relics, my prayers, my goddess – she who held my attention unwaveringly for all these decades.

And of course, there were the compensations.

My beautiful Lady, Catherine had been her name, my Lady Catherine had given me a different outlook on the world, a precious gift that made my days so joyous, spent in wonder, awe and so I had two constant companions in my prison.

A glorious world and the knowledge that one day, I would be close to Catherine again.

Now?

Now I sit wrapped in a bed sheet, and it seems that no time at all has passed since I descended the stairs from the theatre at street level, to the other theatre, way down below and I danced for my Lady Catherine, but she never came.

She never came.

Others came, bright ones, rushing ones, beautiful ones, but none were Catherine.

I could feel that some were very curious and would have liked to know me better, touch me in some way but I refused them all and so I left the theatre with all the others who had found no-one to love then; it was as though we floated up those endless stairs and I was glad, so glad!

It is impossible to understand for anyone but me, but I did not conceive of her not coming to me on that night as any kind slight, or of rejection; I never had any doubt that we were meant to be and it was only a matter of time and she would come to me.

Later, I was contacted by the then Assay of the house of Adela Bach, an old man he was, tired and at the end of his road, and he explained to me the office of Assay and how it was the highest honour to be thus entrusted; he told me that it was my Lady Catherine who had put forward my own name to be successor of his office and I was joyous!

Oh, I was joyous.

I was 19 years old.

When I was 21, the Assay died; and I was formally installed in his position.

Of course, I hoped that she would come for that occasion, but she did not; and yet, it never troubled me, so deep was my conviction that when time was right, she would.

I find myself smiling as I look back upon my young self. I draw the sheet tighter around myself and make the effort to get into bed.

It is far easier this night than it has been in a decade or more.

I lie down and close my eyes.

Yesterday, I was 19.

Now, I am 81.

And Catherine will never come.

Embrace

I lie in the darkness and I feel blessed.

There is no pain in my body, not anywhere.

Pains of many shapes, of many hues and many strands have been my constant companions for so long now, the stillness that is left in their absence is extraordinary. With it comes a wide awareness that I remember – or do I?

Perhaps I never had this level of awareness.

Perhaps I've never felt this sense of peace and of completion.

I think of Catherine, and where before there was just her face and smile, I see more now – I remember her so clearly, but now, I also remember the other details of what I saw, what I felt and what I thought.

For a moment, I wonder whether I had deluded myself for all those years, that she just played me for a fool, I was so young and I knew nothing of love, not a thing.

I knew nothing about myself.

What if she never loved me at all?

What if I was nothing to her, and all these years I lived in absolute delusion, in a hypnotic trance, a puppet that the puppeteer has discarded long ago and so it lies, gathering mould and dust, unmoving, as the days and nights swirl overhead, and as the season turn from one into another ...

Is that all I am?

Is that all I was to her?

Less than nothing at all?

The sensations that arise within me are unknowable, unbearable.

And then from within the darkness that surrounds me there appear two lights, coming from behind, from my left and from my right, I sense them rather than see them, feel them in my body as they become stronger and come closer – I recognise them, those are the two who also walked the stairs to the theatre, who walked with me, walked the same path as me, and they give me courage, and they give me strength.

They come and stand beside me, not to hold me upright like a broken thing, but they stand beside me as fellow warriors would, proud and strong; and this creates a resonance within me which awakens my spirit, and so I stand with them, straight and true; this is not compassion I am being offered here, but a chance to be recognised, to be seen and heard, to regain my self respect and my own purpose, my own path.

Together we stand, and we face the future – it is a wide expansion, full of the unknown; it is wild, it is splendid, and together, we step forward into its embrace.

Stay

I dreamed strange dreams, in a strange state of semi-awareness; I met strange people and yet, they were familiar to me; I exchanged information and knowledge of a kind with those two from downstairs, the pretty young Lady and the other, older one, who looked like a stern general but was nothing of the kind.

They were lovers, so much was clear; yet I did not feel as I though I was intruding, nor did I feel I was unwelcome, or inferior.

As I slowly drifted back into awareness and a bliss of warmth and sublime comfort in body and in mind, it struck me curiously how differently these two had treated me from any of their kind I had encountered across the years.

I wondered how it was, how I was allowed to be here and lie in this bed, in this house, and gain such support, such healing and such friendly attention from the residents.

It was funny, and it was strange.

Standing outside the house, outside the door in the rain and not being able to leave, not being able to do anything but stand and become wetter, and colder; not being able to ring the bell any longer, or hammer on the door; sinking into myself, into my age, my pain, my loneliness and my utter desolation, I thought the end had come.

I knew the end had come.

I knew in all of that that I would never leave this doorstep again, that it was all over, and all would be softened eventually, dissolved, washed away just as the forsaken food parcels were soaking and softening at my feet, eventually they would fall apart and their contents would spill into the cold, blackwet street and so would mine.

I had laid myself finally at their feet, and my heart of hearts, I never really believed that they would come to my aid or care in the slightest.

But they did.

What did that mean?

What had happened?

Why did they order human food, and then failed to collect it?

There was definitely something not right here, for all the benefits the situation had bestowed on me.

A blessing beyond what I had thought could be within the realms of possibilities was my bodily restoration, of which I became aware with force as I attempt to rise, and find it easy, and am not just surprised, but entirely astonished.

There is a large dresser with a mirror above it by the window, and I go to it and look upon myself, perhaps for the first time in years, with critical interest and full attention to detail.

I don't think I look any different, any younger.

Perhaps my eyes are sharper, more focused looking; but that might just be a trick of the light.

My hair is thin, white – old man's hair. My skin is like fragile, ancient manuscripts – old man's skin. Yet I stand with a different posture and there is a different air and as I stand and scrutinise myself in the crystal clear mirror, it is as though the image begins to shift, to ripple – is this just imagination?

But when I concentrate again, it happens again, and it is as though I can see misty shapes weaving around me, around my arms, around my neck and shoulders.

I watch this for a time with absorbed interest, then other needs take precedence.

I wash and find that someone had been in the room in the night – my clothes are spread over the great radiators beneath the bay window and they are all but dry; stiff, wrinkled but serviceable again.

I dress as best as I can and as I do so, I listen with intent but there is not a sound in the house, only the backwash of London traffic kept at bay by the windows. It must be after noon from what I can see, and it is a beautiful, clear day outside.

It is hard to believe that this is the same world outside, pleasant, inviting and golden as the one I experienced last night – entirely unforgiving, black, icy, deadly and without compassion.

153

I am procrastinating.

The Lady whose name I don't know or don't remember told me to leave as soon as I was rested.

I don't want to leave here.

This place is my home, here, with these, that's where my home is, where it has always been since first Catherine unveiled herself to me.

My house is nothing but a waiting post, a temporary shelter, a hotel room where one is sitting and waiting to be called for a performance – I have nothing there I cannot discard more easily than it would take a single thought.

I want to stay here.

Oh dear God, please let me stay.

I don't need a room, I'll sleep in a corner. I'll run your errands and when I cannot run any longer, I'll limp, and then I'll crawl.

Just let me stay ...

As if in answer, a muffled sound drifts through the door and even though it isn't very loud at all, it startles me and breaks me out of my pathetic train of thoughts – what is this?

The sound comes again, and then again, and I realise that it must be the door bell of the house.

Who on Earth would be calling here without being invited?

And was this an opportunity, send to me straight in answer to my prayers to see the young Lady, to be able to plead with her to be allowed to stay?

I pull on my crumpled jacket and make for the door.

Invasion

No-one else seems to be responding to the insistent ringing of the door bell.

I make my way down the stairs and to the surveillance room located at the back of the house. I am relieved and proud in equal measure that I know what to do for I oversaw the installation of this system and had it demonstrated to me, along with many others, at the time.

The cameras show that outside the front door is a middle aged woman in a thick, unflattering winter coat, wearing a woolly hat, who is angrily stabbing at the door bell, alternating with hitting her flat hand against the door and her mouth is moving – she is shouting something.

In the background I see passers by slowing their steps and staring.

This will never do!

I hit the switch that allows me to monitor the microphones.

"I know there's someone in there! Open up or I'll call the police! I mean it! Open up!" the woman is shouting at the top of her voice and hitting the door again.

This is the kind of disturbance that is absolutely unwelcome, and it needs to be dealt with immediately.

I can call certain people and have her be removed; but until then, she needs to quietened. I turn on the speaker phone and say loudly and clearly, "Who are you, and what do you want?"

The woman stops in mid-shout and her mouth is open for a moment as she looks up at the camera above the loudspeaker. Her face is distorted into a balloon by the lens and then her strident voice bursts through the speaker phone, assaulting me, invading the house, "I want to see Steve Burrows. I know you got him in there. I insist on speaking with him, immediately."

Steve Burrows? Never heard of him. But then, what do I know about what has been going on here?

I decide to let her in. I can keep her here until she can be removed, if this should prove necessary.

"Just a moment," I say and press the release button for the outer door.

She pushes it open violently and bursts into the inside room, stops as the second door blocks her steam train progress, pushes at it, looks for a handle.

The outside door closes automatically behind her, and now she is trapped and rendered harmless.

That's what I thought, but then, I am old fashioned in these days. She pulls a mobile phone from her pocket, waves it at the camera and shouts at the top of her voice, "I want to see Steve, and I want to see him right now, or I'm going to call the police. I have them on quick dial, you know!"

I shake my head in defeat, and go to the inner door, release it just as she is about to make the call.

I straighten, look her in the eye and say, "Good afternoon, Madam."

This takes the wind out of her voluminous sails and slowly, she closes the mobile phone and puts it back into her pocket, but does not withdraw her hand from it; it reminds me of someone hiding a gun, ready to use.

The woman is around fifty years of age, with straggling grey hair, overweight, and reminiscent of one of those women one may observe on TV, protesting hunts, motorways and nuclear installations.

On other and many previous occasions, I would have sought to flee such individuals and hide; today, I have no problem holding her on the spot with nothing other than my presence and that is both surprising as well as extremely delightful.

She looks me up and down, looks at the entrance hall and strains to see past me, but she is now uncertain and she says, "I'm looking for Steve Burrows. Is he here? I want to speak with him, urgently."

"Madam," I say with try tones of a well trained butler, "There is no such personage in this house, I assure you."

She looks at me sharply with suspicious small eyes, and before I know it, she has taken a rapid, deep breath and she shouts into the hallway, "Steve! Steve Burrows! Steve! Are you here!"

I am nearly knocked backwards by the sheer volume of her voice and it crashes through the silent house, echoes around the stairwell.

She takes advantage of my moment of vertigo and pushes physically past me, storms towards the bottom of the stairs, places her woolly gloved hand on the banister and shouts again, "Steve! Steve! Are you here! Answer me, Steve!"

And it is then that on the upstairs landing a man appears.

He is clad in black tie, deeply incongruously for the day and time of day, blonde, around 35 years of age and as she sees him, the woman freezes and stares up at him in wide eyed amazement.

He smiles.

"Margaret," he says and now it is his voice, resonant and all encompassing, that fills the hallway absolutely, stilling my breath in a very different way indeed, "How lovely to see you ..."

The Vampire

Over the years, I have had the opportunity to observe a number of their kind, but I have never seen a one like this.

He is radiant, literally luminiscent; as he descends the stairs, he seems to float rather than walk. He is looking down towards the woman Margaret and he is smiling.

On the last step, he stops and extends a hand to the woman who is entirely frozen, entirely entranced; in slow motion and without her will, her own gloved hand rises to meet his.

He takes her hand, then places the other arm around her shoulder and turns her gently.

"Come, let us sit down," he says and I am vibrating from top to toe with the sheer resonance of his voice, even though he speaks most softly.

Then he starts to walk the woman towards the drawing room, looks over his shoulder.

He makes direct eye contact with me and my heart stops.

"You too, Mr Eldrich," he says, no, communicates, commands, implants?

I bow to him but without being able to break eye contact, then he lets me go from his gaze and continues guiding the dishevelled woolly hatted woman down the corridor.

I follow behind, my heart beating now loud and hard, painful in my chest.

I am confused and not a little afraid; I feel out of control and I wish the Lady and the gentleman from last night would be here, so I could know if this was a good thing that was happening, or something that I should have prevented, or never interfered with in the first place.

They had told me to leave but I had stayed, and I had let the woman Margaret in.

The strange couple before me has turned into the entrance to the drawing room and here, Steve Burrows gently deposits the woman on the same sofa I had occupied last night – there is still a dark wet patch in the center where I had been sitting.

The woman folds into herself rather than taking a seat, and her hand is still in Burrow's hand, who is standing in front of her, looking down at her.

I cautiously step into the room and take up station behind the door, and I observe that around his feet, there is indeed a pool of light on the floor, no shadow; he really is glowing, it is not just an impression.

On the sofa, the woman gives a half sob and draws my attention.

"Oh Steve," she says, and I can see tears beginning to slide down her face, "Oh Steve, what has happened to you?"

This causes a ripple in the vampire; it seems as though he is becoming unclear, undefined for a moment; it is just a flashing ripple but when it has passed, he seems very different – much more human, much more physically present and I have to admit relief to notice that he isn't glowing any longer.

The woman and I both let out a breath held for too long and the vampire says, "Margaret," with a very pleasant and loving tone, but in a far more reasonable approximation of a human voice and takes a seat right next to her, still holding her hand encased in that woolly glove, and he turns towards her.

"What brings you here?" he asks her gently.

The woman sniffs and looks at him, lost and helpless, her eyes sliding over his face and hair, small, helpless movements of trying to find familiarity, trying to find answers.

"I thought you were in trouble, again," she said, "I went to your flat, I heard the message on your machine ..."

The vampire nods, then smiles. "I left a trail of breadcrumbs to lead you here, didn't I?" he says gently.

The woman nods, then she withdraws her hand from his, pulls off her gloves and lays them in her lap. When she looks up at him again, her face is serious, concentrated.

It strikes me that she must have loved the man deeply before he became one of them.

How must that be?

What kind of loss must that be?

I have to shake my head.

I cannot know, can't conceive of it.

The woman speaks. "Why are you wearing these clothes," she asks him, urgently and it is clear she is trying to get through to him, trying to reach to the one she used to know, make a connection, recognise him, somehow. "What is this place? Why are you here? Are you on drugs again?" The last statement just slipped out against her will; she colours deeply and looks down at her gloves again.

The vampire who is now in quite perfect disguise and appearing like a man, convincing enough to me but obviously entirely unconvincing to the woman Margaret who knew him from before and loved him well, says gently, "You worry too much, Margaret. I am very happy, and I am not on anything, not now."

She is listening intently, and he goes on to say, "I have made some new friends, that's all."

The woman looks at me still standing by the door and asks incredulously, "You don't mean – him?"

The vampire smiles and replies, "That is Mr John Eldrich. He is an old friend of the family. Mr Eldrich – please come, allow me to make the introductions."

Obediently, I go to stand in front of them, with my hands clasped behind my back, trying to be nonchalant in my crumpled suit, my crumpled shirt, my crumpled skin.

The vampire addresses me.

"Mr Eldrich," he says, "Please meet Margaret Crawley, my most very dear of friends; Margaret, this is Mr John Eldrich."

The woman looks at me curiously, inquisitively and I give a brief bow and hold out my hand to her.

She takes it and shakes it a little too firmly.

"Pleased to meet you – I think ..." she says and then adds, "I am sorry for all the hoopla earlier. I was very worried, I hope you understand ..."

I look into her eyes and think but don't say it, yes. Yes, I understand. I understand that you loved this man very much, that you got involved in a caretaking role, a fire fighting role with little reward apart from a charming smile now and then, that you are like me, one who would do anything to be allowed to be close to something special, something that makes you feel alive when nothing else ever seemed to matter.

The woman tries a smile that fails and we let go off each other's hands, I step back and want to retreat to my corner or perhaps leave the room altogether, but the vampire commands me in gentle, friendly tones, "Please, do join us, Mr Eldrich," and indicates one of the two large arm chairs that face the couch over a low functional coffee table of old oak.

As I sit, I notice that the vampire glances briefly at the ceiling; as he does that, I get a sense of a call that causes a fast streak to shiver down my neck and into my back. I know what that is; I heard it, felt it and understood it – he is calling the others to come and join us here!

My heart beats faster again. I am not sure this is because I am curious to see the Lady again from last night and her husband? lover? companion? or that I am excited by the idea that I can pick up their communications, I can feel and see things I tried to see and feel but I was never able to do that before.

All of this has quite passed Margaret Crawly by without a trace; she is still as I once used to be, on the outside, a child who doesn't understand the double meanings, hears only at the top level, and thus never gains enough information about any situation so it makes a modicum of sense.

She turns back to the vampire and opens her mouth to start speaking again, when the Lady appears in the doorway.

I rise to my feet immediately.

She is truly stunning, much more so than she had been in the night but then, those memories are dark and distant now, and I think of her far more in terms of a loving entity that stood beside me, embraced me and healed me, a warm water wave of sparkling turquoise, rich with nutrients, vibrant with life and strength so freely shared and freely given, than I would think of her as a woman, even though she is unearthly in her beauty, perfection in all her aspects.

Behind her, her companion enters the room and the temperature seems to drop, the light seems to shift.

His age and power radiate right through the sincere attempt to disguise himself as a man; he is a rock, ancient, cold and immensely strong, and I can see that he is frightening the woman Margaret as he would have frightened me if I had not known him as a friend, a fellow warrior come to my rescue, who stood beside me and gladly gave me of his endless strength.

I recognise them both, individually and in combination, the mountains and the sea, green islands dancing with life and bright rushing surf; coral reefs teeming with existence, with unfoldments; that is who they are when they are one and they become far more than just the sum of one, and one.

Yet I am not afraid.

I am in awe, and it is true I can't conceive how someone who should be as little as I am in every way could be within their presence and not crumble to the floor and beg to be a leaf they should deign step upon, to be thus blessed; but above it all, there is the reminiscent resonance of when we stood together, and I wasn't less than they, but welcome, and to both, delight.

The vampire who had once been a man called Steve Burrows tracks my interactions with them both, their response of friendly greeting of an equal who is much appreciated in return and he seems pleased.

He smiles.

He moves closer on the sofa to the woman who is absolutely speechless now and at a loss at what to think or even feel, and places a protective arm about her shoulder.

"Alexandra! Gaius! How delightful to see you here today," he says and then his composition as a man begins to waver, cracks and splits seem to appear within the shell of man he had assumed and from these cracks bright light is cascading, bright light with opalescence playing, radiating out and in the slowest motion of a mermaid's hair in water, these strands of living, liquid light begin to

162

seek and find, and reach and touch us all – first Margaret, then Alexandra, then the man he had called Gaius and finally, they reach me.

Oh!

What a sensation!

It is electric, it is vibrant, it is a touch that travels all around me and then finds connections, flows inside me, warms me up and at the same time, catapults me up, fast and high, into a different level of awareness altogether – oh!

I am still here, right here in this room, in this chair; I am still here and I am absolutely aware that I am, but overlaid and at the same time, there is so much more – a universe of more, a multidimensional fish tank where we are shifting shapes and there are so many others here as well, other things, other existences; shadows and resonances from above and below reaching here as well as everything there is already – oh!

The vampire speaks.

He transmits and it is simply fantastic to see how banded colours stream across the various layers, turning into doves or wings that touch and move existences, objects, cause many floating beings to divert their paths, this way and that; it is impossibly complex but it doesn't frighten me because it is all responsive, all connected and it makes perfect sense to me now, when before, I saw only a few hints, clues, and it was never enough to make a bigger picture, or to formulate a plan.

"We are near complete," the vampire informs us.

"Welcome our brother and our sister."

On the level where there is just a room with furniture, with windows and a fire place, carpets and light fitting, where two people seem to stand by the door, two seemed to be sitting on the couch and a fifth was reclining in an armchair, it is as though from nowhere, another man arrives – he materialises to my left, he is also wearing formal black tie evening dress, a young man of perhaps 25 years of age – I recognise this one! This one is called Mark Edwards and I used to deal with him, many, many years ago, fifty years or more? He used to

163

be my contact to the house. I always thought him charming and disarming in his shyness and sincerity; I remember missing him when another took his place and I am frankly delighted to see him here today.

The vampire on the couch points towards the fire place to my right, and there appears an exquisitely beautiful young woman of oriental descent; her appearance closes a circle that we are forming in this room, and which has now become complete.

3: Xiao Hong

Of Music & Portals

When I was still Arada, I really didn't think that I should ever know a state more blessed than this.

I drifted in comfort and absolute protection; I dreamed and learned; there was no harshness, and there was no fear.

It was not until I was there and all the fear had finally left me that I understood just how my previous existence had been blighted in that way.

I was always so afraid.

I wasn't afraid of anything in particular – perhaps that is not true, I was terrified of my father, of my grandfather, of my mother, of my grandmother, of my teachers, especially so.

But even if they weren't there, the few short moments when I would escape into the solitude of forest or of rain, I was still terrified only I didn't realise it.

I was inside a whole world of fear and thus I never recognised it for what it was.

The only thing that would sometimes lift me up and out of this endless suffering was music.

I would listen to music, and I would listen hard, tried to find the essence behind the notes, and the silences that lay between them, for I thought I could perceive a doorway there, a portal through which I might step and leave myself behind, rise fresh and new and become something other than what I was – a terrified nothing, a nothing that fails to please, and thereby, is worse than nothing.

When I first was taught to play the flute, I thought that this might be a magical thing, a device that would open up those doorways for those who would play the right notes, in the right order; but then, they made me play these tunes that weren't that, and somehow, the better I became at mimicking exactly what they wanted to hear, the further away my freedom and my joy of music seemed to become.

Still, I worked hard for fear of causing disappointment, for fear of punishment and I was amongst those who were chosen to play some pieces at an afternoon soiree in a museum.

That is where I saw him for the first time, that's where I found my salvation.

There was a young man standing quietly in the shadow of one of the large pillars in the museum's entrance hall.

I played only for him.

I played to him.

I made my own melody on that day, told him all about me, and the teacher who was conducting us was horrified, and all the others in the group were too, but they kept on playing their notes, and I sang for help with everything I had, I turned that flute into a dozen war horns, calling re-enforcements, mayday, mayday, save my soul.

When the piece ceased, there was a moment of timeless silence and then the applause of the bystanders engulfed us like artillery fire and I couldn't hear what the teacher was saying to me, screaming at me, his mouth was wide open and his face torn into ribbons of hatred as he dragged me by the arm of the podium and shoved me away.

The audience was still applauding as the man stepped forward, entirely oblivious of my teacher and with eyes only for me, and then everything fell away, the noise, the surroundings, everything, and he held out his hand to me.

I took it and he led me away.

I must have dropped the flute somewhere along the line, I don't remember, and from that moment forth, there was only he and his world, he and his word, now and forever.

Mark Edwards.

I went back to my family and yet I did not.

I received beatings but I never felt them; they shouted at me, my mother cried, and none of it was real, and all there was for me were my meetings with him, when we would sit in the park by the lake, rain or shine, and he would tell me about his kind, and about his world, and prepare me for the transition.

166

By the time the night of nights came, my parents weren't beating me any longer; as I got dressed for the occasion, my father told me that if I left, I could never come back and would no longer be their daughter. My mother and grandmother cried and pleaded; then they screamed as well yet I was tranquil in every way, unseeing of them, my eyes and mind tuned to far horizons, and shivering with excitement.

I walked to the theatre.

As I came close, I noted that there were others like me, walking like I did, and we were heading in the same direction.

When I turned the corner into the street where the theatre lay, I saw even more, and we were all streaming towards the entrance where two men calmly stood and smiled at each of us and all of us as I raised my skirt to step up and into the entrance hall.

There were many of us, and although no-one spoke, I felt a great kinship and friendliness with everyone. We were all beautiful, and in love.

Filing into the auditorium, not taking a seat but going straight down the middle towards the stage, I am not a spectator tonight, I am the event, we all are. My heart beats higher as I step up to the stage, and then we walk across the stage and into the back, backstage, yes, that is where reality is happening, and here is the entrance to the real world, the real reason why we came.

"The curtains at the back of the stage will be open," Mark told me and even though I was entirely lost in his eyes, in his voice, in presence I still listened, and I remembered everything he said. "You will simply walk through a hallway that lies behind the stage, and then you come to a great golden arch, and that is the entrance to the stairwell that will take you to the underground theatre."

I saw it then and when I saw it with my own eyes, it isn't a surprise; but everything is greater, richer and there are no words that can describe the truth of being there.

I had searched for a portal – here it was, and it was real.

With every gentle, slow long step on that enormous stairway down and into the real theatre, my life and all my fears, all my hopes and dreams and every petty memorance of all that faded, it faded more and more, and by the time I emerged into that fantastic realm so far below, crimson and gold, precious and vibrant with sensations I had bloomed into something I had never known that I might dare hold up for all to see.

I had unfolded.

Radiantly and gladly, I let the music stream to me, let it enchant me, let it invite me to reveal myself, further and further, all and everything, I am precious, I am young, and I am here ...

And then, I saw and felt the masters, these others, they came and they danced with us, danced with me, and each one was a delight, each one was different; none of them made me afraid, not one amongst them, not even the oldest, or the darkest.

Many came until there was a one who touched me and to whom I resonated in a whole new way; I shook and trembled, and it was as though leaves fell from me, revealing my inner core and it was ready, it was willing and it wanted to receive this one in preference to all the others.

My Lord had come.

My one true Lord and master, my re-creator and my lover – my Lord Meruvian had chosen me.

Breath On A Cold Morning

How can I describe the bliss of the first union?

I cannot.

I have not words for this, nor tunes to bring the resonance of this into a world where others might then share it; there are no colours and no lines upon a canvas or a sheet of pale rice paper who could capture all that wonder.

The more he took from me, the more I needed him to take; I wanted him to take it all, I wanted him to have it all, to have my soul and all that I would have to give.

He took but slowly and the pleasure was excruciating; it was an agony the like I've never known and neither have I known an agony so sweet and yes I wished that it should never end.

But end it did as end it must; when there was next to nothing left to give, it was then that he took me even closer still and nourished me from his own essence and now, I must not speak for even an attempt to frame, approximate that first transfusion of my own Lord's splendour, of his being can be nothing but an insult to the holiness of what it was.

I was drinking love, and it was love that changed me, made me go to sleep and there, to start my transformation.

"You will sleep for a long time," Mark had told me on a frosty cold morning, and his breath had not created a plume of steam as mine did still, and I held my breath because I didn't want to be like this, but liked to play pretend like a small child, pretend that I was just like him.

"You will sleep, and you will dream. We will come to you and we will feed from you, but every one will give you of themselves in return, so you will slowly change until you are like us. And then, you will awaken."

"And I will be like you ..." I said and there was the plume of white that confused my words, or carried them.

Mark looked at the white and at the words and smiled.

"Yes," he said tenderly, "You will be just like me, a Cestra, and you too will speak with those like you are now, and tell them of our world."

He wasn't to know that what he promised wouldn't come to pass.

Unstoppable

Being Arada is an exquisite experience.

It is a state of complete acceptance; it is a kind of unconsciousness that has awareness but it doesn't ask, or question, or demand.

There is a sense of warmth, protection and beauty; and then, they come.

When they come, I don't awaken but the dream shifts, becomes different; richer, more sensuous.

When they come, they are hungry and I know that they are.

One will come to me and make themselves known, and I can feel their hunger; it causes an echo in myself, a fullness, a desire to discharge, a need to find release. Their hunger and my need circle each other, dance with one another, weave into each other, tempting, tantalising, drawing it out and making it ever more sensuous, excruciatingly exquisite until we give into it and touch, reach deeply into one another and hunger and need turn into a single flow, a charge of fiery delight, delicious, incredibly delicious and entirely intoxicating.

I can feel them controlling themselves; controlling me; sometimes, there is a sense of another or more than one far away and always, I beg for more, deeper, faster – take me!

But they hold me in their merciless, excruciating ecstasy and drain me slowly and never quite completely; and they leave me just enough of themselves so that I can re-build myself around what they have left, and I need to use their residue to make that happen.

I sleep again, I rest again, and I dream, new dreams, new information, with every exchange and every taking, my dreams expand and they become more real, more lucid.

Mark told me, "Being Arada is a kind of apprenticeship. You learn everything about us then, because in a union, it is not just life force that is exchanged, but also knowing."

I sat on a park bench in the rain and nodded seriously.

Oh, how I had no idea what the reality of this would be like, what it would entail!

It is as well that I did not, for if I had, I think I would have thrown myself at Mark Edwards and forced him into a full union, there and then – rape on a park bench!

And talking about rape, and remiscences, so the time has come to think about what happened when the other came to me.

I was more than ready for another union at the time.

My dreams were vibrant, full of powerful ocean waves, deep and green; I was vibrant and ready for union.

I felt someone coming, and I felt a strange sensation – I did not know this one, did not recognise them and further, they did not seem to share the same familiar resonance that did exist in me and all the others here.

He was a stranger, and he was not just hungry, but veritably starving.

He was ferocious and he did not dance with me.

He was simply there and he took me, without hindrance, without restraint and I felt as though finally, my prayers had been answered and I could follow my true nature at last.

As much as he tore straight into me, I threw myself at this stranger with a desperation and a force that left me astonished; and the union was insane, uncontrollable, fantastic – and unstoppable.

Inside The White

When I awoke in the white, I thought I might have died.

Then I wondered who that I was that I thought might have died, and then, who the I was who was wondering about such things.

I was confused.

It was very difficult to know anything inside this white, and it was beautiful and endlessly interesting with tiny stars being born here and there from the denseness of this light, flashing up and out and then disappearing; new ones arising in new positions; over and over.

But it was the white that made the first connection – I remembered the plumes of steam from my mouth, and then I remembered another who did not breathe out in white, and when I did, I became aware that this other was present here.

I remembered the other, and because of that, I remembered myself.

One thing connected to another, and yet another, weaving upwards, sideways; knowings, memories and other forms of awareness, all of that began to combine to something and finally, it all fitted together and I was ...

I am Xiao Hong. When I was little, I wanted my hair to be golden like the palest winter sun, thick and flowing like the rippling waves of wind on fields of gold; my eyes to be round like a cow's, pale porcelain blue diamonds, and my name should be Samantha. I would have a lovely voice that makes everyone silent and the birds sing a harmony when I speak. I would be a princess and no-one would dare deny my every wish.

I am in green land, bright green grass all around, forward, backward, left and right, to all the horizons, and the sky above is blue, without a cloud, without a sun.

I look around and I see that I am not alone.

There are two others here, two beings, and I know them both.

The first is Mark, or what I thought of as Mark when I knew him in that way.

The other is the hungry stranger.

There seems to be a great distance between us and as I regret this should be so, the distance decreases with a fast rushing and we are close together, standing in a triangle, close enough so we could hold hands if we extended our arms.

"I am Xiao Hong," I say as though it was necessary.

Mark nods and clears his throat before saying, "I am Mark Edwards."

The hungry stranger, a skinny white man with thin fair hair and piercing blue eyes says, "And I am Steve Burrows."

For a moment, the green grass dream drops away as I realise that I know exactly what that means, who he is, who he has been, and every single moment of his time, as though it was my own.

I rush through all of that in fast spiralling turns, down, sideways, through and out; a multi-dimensional gallery of images, feelings, sensations, sounds and voices, thoughts, nightmares and confusions, symbols – and then I'm out the other side and back where I was, standing with the other two in a place of dreams.

I turn to Steve Burrows in preference and I address him.

"You and I completed a union. I know you now, entirely."

He nods. "I know you, and I hold you," he responds.

For a moment, I am confused but then, I understand. I have no longer a body. It burned in the union, and I am now entirely transformed – but not in the way Mark had told me about, or how it was supposed to be.

Mark speaks. "I too completed the union with Steve," he says. "At this time, he holds us both."

I look down at myself and spread my arms, extend my fingertips.

I am aware that this is not a body in the sense of what I was used to, but it looks like the body I used to have, and it responds in a very similar fashion.

"Am I dead?" I ask, uncertain all of a sudden.

Mark and Steve shake their heads in unison, and in unison they reply, "You are transformed."

"Am I – a ghost?"

Mark responds to this alone.

"Yes, you could say that. But you have the ability to manifest in physicality. Normally, you would have learned this step by step in the last stages of Arada, Arada Ta Cestra. It would have been easier because your new body would have inhabited the same physical location as your old one did, and of course, there would have been many to aid you in your first emergence."

Steve Burrows says, "There is no need for that. Just show her."

I look from him to Mark and immediately understand what he means by that.

And I am immediately excited.

I have been wanting a union with this one ever since first we met; not one of those cautious Arada-Cestra unions under strict supervision, but that rushing, intense insanity of a full union without any safeguards, without any holding back.

Mark is similarly excited by the idea, but he has much old entrainment; and he is afraid.

I understand that. I am an expert in afraid – I have my spent my mortal life in just that state of indecision, as any decision might lead to doing wrong, and thus straight into doom and suffering.

I understand his fear, but I also understand that his fear is unfounded, and that is based on teachings of the old – he had teachers too, just as I used to have, and even though they did not rap his knuckles with a bamboo cane, but spoke most softly and insistently, the end result is just the same.

I turn to Steve Burrows. He looks straight at me, and I know that he won't act as a master, or a teacher; it is as though he's telling me, "I took you because I wanted you, and that is what I did. What you do, that is up to you."

So I re-focus on Mark.

I've always wanted him, wanted to taste him, wanted to touch him, wanted to take him and make him my own, or give myself to him entirely; who knows, it might be just the same.

He is beautiful. Even his fear smells and tastes delicious, tiny red strands escaping from his chest, from his throat. I call to one of

175

these and make it come to me; I open my mouth and it lands on the tip of my tongue, tingles through and through me, awakens my hunger – I am fully aware, I am fully here and I am fully manifest; my clarity increases tenfold and now I see all the colours, the weaving connections and the powerful, deep inner pulses, the waves at the core of his being – I want that.

I want you.

Come to me.

His fear crests but so does his need for release and for union; both crash against each other, cancel each other out, and helplessly, he lies before me.

I flow forward and simply envelop him, hold him close and begin to feed from him, begin to drink deeply, hungrily, and finally he lets himself go and falls to me, releases himself to me and we fall into a wild and rushing starburst of ecstasy, instantaneous discharges caught and fed into a furnace fire that glows brighter and more brightly still until –

We emerge on the side of each other, free and clear, and we turn around and we are astonished.

We completed a full union, and we emerged unscathed, no, better, better, so much better, by so far!

I am me and him, and he is him and me – I know his days and he knows mine; and we are both relieved of our pressures and of our hungers all the same; we are clear, we are delighted, we are empowered and it is then, we laugh and dance in sheer delight.

Burrows grins.

"Told you so," he says.

I Fly

It is fantastic.

I am so wide awake, so ultra aware. I can feel – everything!

I can sense, I can see until eternity and I can choose!

I laugh aloud and shift and ripple, I become Samantha of my dreams, the alter ego and it is both nothing, as well as everything; it stills and fills a need and when that need has gone, I feel a rising and a growing, and I am a dragon, fluid, swift and fire bright inspired – I must rise, and I must roar and laugh!

I paint delightful spirals straight into the sky, I paint my name and my existence and my joy is such that it infects the others and they too turn into dragons and they join me in my dance.

We weave and rush around each other, chase each other, circle here and there and finally we find a new delight in matching our paths and our purposes; it is natural and obvious that we should draw together, closer and more closely still until we cease to be three, and instead, we are one and the same, the greatest of all dragons in the sky.

I am the greatest of all dragons in the sky.

And so I fly and celebrate my own existence, so at home and not just here but everywhere, a welcome aspect of a greater picture that was never quite complete until I made my entrance here.

I fly.

I fly and learn, absorb what lies about me like so much plankton, take that nourishment that truly is in everything into my own deep structure and find it powering me, renewing me, and changing me ...

It is wonderful and I can be like this forever, I can be forever.

Then, from far, far away, so far away that it might be beyond the end of all, and long before there was beginning, I perceive a call.

It is specific; it is alien; it is meant for me.

For me?

An aspect of an aspect resonates and draws towards the call, pulls strongly, and we follow with that movement, with what could be a desire or attraction, but it changes our path.

We spiral down and further down, far out and down, and further still until we reach a level where we are no longer one alone. Instead, we are a group of three and it is one of us that hears and heeds this calling; I am simply on this journey as a visitor or perhaps more; as we go down and further down and old things come to me from days and times when there were days, and names, and singular existences I then begin to recognise that Mark and I are with Steve Burrows as he dives and sweeps, prepares to land and manifest in physicality.

Delicious

Have you ever hovered in the back of someone else's mind and observed as they act, and move?

It is a very strange state of affairs.

It took me a while to recognise the house, my own view of it was different and my memories very displaced; I had been here in various states of high confusion and the rest of the time, the last 30 years I have been asleep in the Underworld.

Steve is speaking and acting, and Mark and I are observing.

I feel that we are a tall crystal pyramid that could rotate at any time and show a different facet instead of the one that is being presented; I actually feel a desire for rotation and as though this state of only showing the facet that is Steve requires determination and a counter movement to be employed to keep him there and both of us away and back.

I am aware of everything that happens, and below me is a reservoir of tremendous knowing of so many things that I did not experience myself, yet it is at my disposal and it helps me make sense of the occurrence, the individuals and the reasons for their combinational appearances at this time, in this place.

At some point, Steve and Mark commune and arrive at the conclusion that we should manifest separately, not least to show those who are here that we are still around, that we haven't died, that we are very well indeed.

This is exciting.

I wonder fleetingly if I will know what to do, remember how to do this from these places where the other's knowledges are in our shared sub structure; but before I have even finished wondering, Steve has set a process in motion that takes me, sweeps me up and out and deposits me in the room in a tingling state of awareness and surprising cohesion.

Ah but this is too intriguing, too delicious!

I can feel muscles in my face tense and tighten as I start to smile; I have no muscles in my face and these must be resonance memories, feedback devices left from the old days and that makes me smile even more. I flutter my lids for the sheer sensation and the effect of making that level of impressions in the room appear and disappear, like an old film played at the wrong speed; my hands seek and find my side, my hips.

I giggle out aloud and the others in the room turn to me.

Mark and Steve are both grinning broadly; they are resonant and feel what I feel just the same. I recognise Alexandra, who had come to me many times when I was still Arada and we have a strong bond; I resonate to her and she picks up and transmits from me to the old one who is by her side; so a web is woven between all five of us through which information and state are being transmitted smoothly and with perfect clarity.

I am fascinated by the old one and make myself known to him in preference.

There are levels and layers to him that remind me of my first Lord, my first love, Lord Meruvian. It is his age, I'm sure; he has a depth that none of us here have achieved as yet, and it makes his tastes and textures curiously rich and deeply satisfying. I flow to him, I cannot stop myself – I want a union, I want to know if I can match or regain what once there was with my Lord Meruvian, and for which in truth, I hunger deeply still.

The old one, on his part, is very curious and quite delighted by my aspects and the newness of my being; he comes forward to meet me and we are just about to touch when there is a groundswell raising, a wave that not exactly comes between us but it asks respectfully that we should not engage right now, but to delay; it draws my attention to the other two presences in the room, and these are human, vulnerable, and confused.

The knowing stands in our resonant web that there will be time for each of us to know each other and experience each other; draw together and become a single force, that it is ordained and we are here exactly for that reason; for now, and on another plane, there is some work which still remains to be accomplished.

180

There is no regret as I agree with this assessment and exchange a playful touch with the old one, Gaius, "I look forward to tasting you when the time is right ..."

And so it is that all five of us turn our attention to below and to the two who are the latest members of our house, they just don't know it yet.

4: John Eldritch

Starburst

There are five vampires in the room, one distraught and terrified woman, and then, there is me.

I am standing in a circle with these others and I still can't get used to the idea that I should be welcome here, that I am in all actuality a part of what is happening here. But I am, I can feel it; I know it and it makes the hair at the back of my neck rise.

There is a silence when Edwards and the Chinese girl arrive, simply materialise; but this silence is a cacophony of events flying backwards and forwards; a veritable storm of interaction is taking place here and I am only aware of this at the most outside of levels.

The Chinese girl vampire giggles out aloud; and this shifts everything. I can see Edwards and the blond vampire starting to smile as well as though these three were sharing a secret joke, but then the smile spreads to the Lady by the door and her lover, previously stern and steady, seems to melt and smile with a very sensuous aspect as well.

Oh damn, I wish I was in on that joke!

Oh damn this, I wish I had been chosen!

The Lady speaks.

"You have been chosen, John," she says and I am immediately entirely captivated by her and yet aware that she is speaking in an official capacity, on behalf of the entire group of vampires.

"This is a time of tremendous change," she says slowly and deliberately, addressing herself entirely to me. In her voice, I feel as though I can hear echoes of the others, speaking in unison. It is fascinating, frightening, and yet I am deeply honoured by the attention they should give to me. In the back of my mind, a hope begins to awaken.

It is an old hope, one that I have carefully laid to rest, buried in a deep casket made of perfect steel, buried deep down below and not even a grave stone to mark its place of rest, but even though it was contained in that way, it never ceased to be.

It is the hope that I should be like them – not to age, not to be in pain, to be beautiful like them, to be immortal.

I could not afford to carry that hope with me as I got older and as the years passed by and I was nothing but a servant, and I would be nothing but their servant, just like old Mr Peterson who died in their service, and who had only me to sit with him when he did.

I realise that there are many things that I have buried deep.

I remember holding his thin hand of fragile twigs and autumn leaf skin, cold it was and it wouldn't warm, it drew the warmth from my own hand, and I wasn't looking at him, I was looking at the door and praying that one of them would come, and do something. To stop him from dying, to take his pain away, to bless him, or something.

No-one came, and old Mr Peterson took a long time to die. I stayed with him until the end. I oversaw his funeral at which there was only me and the undertakers, and the only words that were spoken were, "Rest in peace."

It was in December he died, around the time of Solstice; the Festival of Blessings, they call it, and I stood at Mr Peterson's grave and I stood at my own grave, just the same.

It wasn't as though they ever promised anything else than that.

They didn't lie to me, gave me any illusion, any false hope in word or action.

But the hope remained.

I could not kill it, no matter how I tried.

So all I could do is to bury it deep and tried to forget.

And here she stands, the Lady, and she speaks with a voice of many, and she says, "You have been chosen."

Tears are streaming freely down my face as from the deepest inside of me, the buried hope, perhaps my buried soul begins to flare and shake the foundations of me, bursts through the barriers, crashes out of its confinement and blows apart the cemetery at the center of my being.

The hope flares high and wide and bright and I know that it touches them all, that it blesses them all and showers them in gratitude, that it is my payment for their kindness, their acceptance, for their decision to spare me that fate I thought was mine for all this time.

I can feel them touching the flaring sun at the center of my being, I can feel them being drawn to it, I can feel them coming close and wanting to know of it, asking me for more, to give them what I am, and one last time, I ask the question, "Do you really want me?" and I receive a fivefold affirmation, a fivefold invitation, and so I let myself fall back, release the last restraints and let myself explode at last, and so I die in one extraordinary starburst that has waited all my life to come to pass.

Phoenix

I stand in the room with the others. On the sofa, the woman Margaret has fainted and lies as if asleep, her head supported in Steve Burrow's lap. He has taken the woolly hat off and is stroking the woman's grey hair with long, pale fingertips that are entirely of light in essence and yet real enough to straighten her tangled hair, making it smooth, making it flow over her head, over her neck.

It is a beautiful scene; he has such love for her.

When she will join us, and it won't be long, she will be able to see this, as I see it; it will help her make that transition smooth between the then, and her new futures, whatever they may be.

I am tranquil.

Around my feet, there lies a pile of ashes, white silver grey, slightly sparkling.

This is what my body has become.

Ashes to ashes, dust to dust.

Arada dust.

Fairy dust.

Mark Edwards comes towards me and places his hand on my arm.

My arm?

My arm is on the floor, in pieces.

"No it isn't," Xiao Hong says gently in her sweet voice, she sounds like birds at the beginning of the day. "This is your arm, this is your body. It is all new."

I look at my arms and my hands. They are just the same as I remember them, I'm even wearing the same crumpled suit I was wearing when I was still – alive?

"You are alive," says Edwards and he smiles at me, moves his head to the side and down to catch my eyes, "You are very much alive."

I have to smile back at him because he is right. I am very much alive indeed. I feel more alive right now than I ever have,

I look at my old hands and the crumpled suit sleeve again. Can I do this? I feel the others surreptitiously sliding a little closer, lending me a helping hand; I can see myself from their perspective, all different angles, and the first thing I try to do is to straighten the suit, but as I do, a memory takes over of the favourite suit I've ever owned, hand made in Seville Row, a navy blue pinstripe suit that somehow made me feel better dressed than anything else I've ever worn.

I waver and ripple just slightly and I can see in the many visions, many mirrors of myself in the eyes of the others that the suit becomes; it becomes with a perfect matching shirt and tie and waistcoat; the shoes and socks as well, that makes me smile even more.

But it doesn't quite fit.

It doesn't belong to this old man, it belongs to another, another me from another time and even as I think it, I become it and I am stunned to feel the feelings that I felt when I was that – in my prime, no longer awkward with the limbs of youth, walking in power and in confidence, feeling at home inside my self and quite invulnerable, safe.

The whole experience shifts me into an elder state but that dissolves into the then and now as well, and a merging happens that makes me one and the same – I am old and I am young, I am vampire and I am human, I am – just me.

I make the movement of taking a deep breath and look up from my new manifestation at the assembled group, and all of them bow and smile; there is a feeling of applause in the air, of being proud of my accomplishment, and being happy for me that I managed to do this thing, which now I know would take a Cestra decades to perfect.

I really and truly have become one of them.

No Choice

In the drawing room, the vampires are socialising.

Gaius and Xiao Hong are flirting; he is leaning against a dresser by the window and she is standing before him, small and frail, exquisite. They are playing with one another, getting to know one another.

Steve is still sitting with the unconscious woman on the sofa; Alexandra sits in the far right corner, opposite me, and Mark Edwards has taken the other armchair to my left. We are simply interacting, becoming comfortable with each other across the levels, and in many ways, I am sure this is designed to help me settle into all of this.

As I look around and let the conversations, communications and alignments unfold without as yet taking a direct part in any of these, I become aware that it's not just about me.

It is about all of us.

I didn't realise that Steve Burrows had himself been entirely human only a few short days ago when I first saw him; I didn't know that everyone had thought that he had killed Xiao Hong, or that Mark Edwards had been catapulted into being the leader of this house in an equally short time span.

Every one of us has been through a major transformation, and we all need time to settle, even Gaius; a strange and ancient vampire who just happened to pass by and got caught up in the whirlpool of unfoldments here.

Unfoldments. What a strange word that is, why I did I choose that word?

Ah ... of course. The Covenant. The vampire's bible and their law. My law! I laugh to myself and shake my head. I don't know about the others, but I am far from settled in all of this, and I deeply appreciate the time we are spending, simply being here, in these comfortable, soothing surroundings which indicate a sense of home, of belonging.

Alexandra heard me laugh and asks me, "How are you feeling, John," which is nothing more but an opening to a form of energy exchange, if truth be known.

"I am feeling very well, thank you," I say and I really do want to append to that statement, "My Lady," but of course, Alexandra knows this and she laughs in delight. Steve and Mark pick the vibration up and both laugh as well.

Steve says, "You can call her that if you want to. It is nothing but the truth."

Alexandra smiles, looks down but is clearly pleased; it is fascinating and in a way, extremely delightful that in spite of everything, we are still all really very human, in many ways.

Mark says, "This is something I have always found surprising. How – human – we all still are. Even my Lady Adela ..." and there, he becomes wistful, saddened.

His sadness touches me deeply; his longing strikes me deeply and I am confounded for a moment that I should feel so intimately for another, but it also connects me to him more deeply, and it makes me want to alleviate this, help him, support him.

I feel a strange sensation then, and I realise that I am falling in love with Mark, with all of them. With every moment that passes, with every thing I learn about myself and every one of these, our relationship gets closer, more intimate, more profound.

Is this a good thing?

Into my mind whispers the Covenant.

The first law is love.

It is a good thing.

Oh, but it is.

Steve speaks softly. "Will you invite the Lady Adela to join us here?"

Alexandra looks to him swiftly, then across to Mark and says in a rush, "Oh Mark! Oh Mark please do! I miss my Lady and I wish she was here with us, right now!"

Mark Edwards looks shocked, then pained. He places a hand to his temple, shakes his head. His shoulders drop and he says quietly, "She is Ferata now. She is unreachable."

Steve sits up. Quite sharply, he says, "She is reachable. You know her. We can find her, anywhere, in any state, and we can bring her here."

Across the room, Gaius and Xiao Hong break off their conversation and come forward to join us.

Gaius says, "I have no doubt that this can be done, and I have no doubt remaining that the Ferata stage is just as much a waste of time as all the others are. There is no reason to spend centuries as rocks and trees, not now."

His presence and his voice is shocking in its depth and resonance; he is an amazing being and I deeply drawn to him, to his knowledge and his wisdom; but as I follow with this drawing even faintly, it does not lead me towards him but instead, it leads me into me, for I have gained all that when we exchanged ourselves, when I exchanged myself with all of them and gave them me, and in return, they gave me what they are.

This is inconceivable. I cannot be like ... him ...

Mark is shocked by Gaius's statement. He says nothing but he is clearly unhappy, and it is Steve who says to him, quite gently but with much authority, "Mark, your dedication to do the right things and follow the laws, such as you knew them, is commendable. But I think you will find, if you look inside yourself, that the way you are feeling right now is based on an old state that has now gone. I think you should go and find the Lady Adela, bring her home to us. I believe it will finally cure you of the misinformation, and the hold the old rules still have on you."

Mark is contemplating this and what it would entail, then Alexandra speaks and ask, "What of Satari? I miss my Cestra sister. Can she rejoin us now?"

I search for information on the topic and find it easily and clearly. A beautiful dark young maiden with the liquid eyes of a deer, Alexandra's friend and Cestra sister. Gaius took her and placed her into a stable house when all was falling apart here and she was too frightened to continue.

Steve and Gaius speak in unison, a double resonance that creates the effect of sounding like an oracle, a message from above, "She is resting. We should leave her be."

"Whose house is this now?" I ask and I am confounded by the sound and the experience of thus having spoken in this group.

Alexandra looks to Steve for an answer, Mark looks to Gaius, Xiao Hong looks to Mark and Gaius looks at me and smiles.

I think loudly, *All together now* ... and we all say it at the same time, an amazing theatrical chorus that makes the windows vibrate, "This is our house."

Then we all laugh and I lie back in this armchair without having a body and just let the situation be, don't try to think or analyse this any further, for what good would it do?

Mark says, "I will do it. I will seek and find the Lady Adela, and I will bring her back to join us. We shall all go to the festival together. The house of us."

We send affirmation and delight that he has come to this decision.

I have another question.

"What of Margaret here?"

Steve answers immediately.

"If there is one living human I would want to be here with me and share this, it is her. She is a wonderful person, true, trustworthy, so much more than she thinks herself to be. I would not want to leave her behind. That is why I called her to be here. I will transform her and then she shall join us as an equal."

We acknowledge and respect his decision, but I do have to ask.

"Will you give her any choice in the matter?"

Steve looks across the table, straight at me, and I know that he will not; that there is no choice. Even if he was to present her with the options, and ask for her opinion, it would still not be a choice, for she simply could not say "No" to the proposal or walk away.

I nod and acknowledge fully, when Gaius asks, "How will you accomplish the transformation?"

A fast smile streaks across Steve's lips and there is a definite sense of mischievousness about him; it is something about him that is refreshing, and attractive, something that makes him very different from the rest of us.

He leans forward and gently takes the unconscious woman by the shoulders, straightens and lifts her, lays her against the back of the sofa where her head just falls to one side.

He arranges her until her position is stable, then he turns to me and flashes me a brief look before slowly and with great care, turning her head so it is facing away from him. He brushes her hair away, pulls her scarf from her coat and thus has exposed her neck.

A tremendous sense of amusement comes from him as he slowly bends down and then seems to bite her in the neck in the classic Hollywood vampire style – I see that he has indeed, bitten right into her energy system, created a great breach and her life force is flowing straight into him, a tumbling cascade of all the colours of the rainbow pouring fast and faster into Steve who absorbs it just as fast and it is not more than just a few seconds later, and the woman's shape collapses right into itself and all of her, her clothes and everything, has totally disintegrated and now drifts in tiny sparkles down and onto the floor, onto the couch, revealing the space that once she occupied.

It was absolutely fascinating to me to experience the reactions of everyone to this event.

I personally was partially amused, partially jealous and partially dismayed that Steve Burrows would do something as dramatic as that with such nonchalance, and as though it was absolutely nothing – a brief TV sketch, an imitation of the vampire myth for his own amusement. Should there not have been more ceremony? More preparation? Should the woman not at least have been awakened and at least a show of co-operation attempted?

Mark Edwards is absolutely shocked and perfectly horrified. Gaius is very amused and there is something that he knows about this situation which doesn't seem to be common knowledge – I wonder what it might be?

192

Alexandra is actually scared and tries to withdraw; Xiao Hong on the other hand, is giggling at Steve's vampire impression and sees no problem in Margaret's instantaneous dispatchment from life, to afterlife.

Steve is still leaning forward, across a now empty space. He is glowing again, pulsating, charged, electric. He brings out his hand and traces the silver dust on the sofa with an outstretched fingertip, then he lifts his hand and points – the silver dust begins to rise as though it was magnetically drawn to his finger, from the sofa and from the floor, it streams up towards him and he straightens, pulls his arm back and now a complete train, a veil of dust follows his movements. He weaves it here and there and we are all completely transfixed by this his manipulation of material matter, watching the sparkling dust behave like a flock of tiny birds on a still winter day, with one mind, with his mind; it forms into a wavering oval, then into a circle that becomes denser and denser, smaller and smaller, tighter and tighter; as it contracts more and more, it becomes brighter too until it is a tiny star that floats in mid air. Steve drops his hands and closes his eyes. The star travels slowly towards him, then it enters his forehead straight between his eyebrows and disappears.

A smile travels through the entire man from head to foot; he smiles and when he opens his eyes to find us all staring at him, he says, "That was absolutely delicious."

Alexandra slides off the edge of the couch and sidles around the room, around behind my chair and until she is close to Mark's, there she sits down, close to his knee, like a child would seek the protection of her father.

It is Gaius who addresses them both.

"The wilderness is a fantastic place," he says and although his words do not make sense to me at the conscious level, they soothe me most profoundly, as though the room was filled with fragrance of elder forests, slow life, immutable and perfect, silent, full of grace.

"Don't be afraid of it. It holds treasures like we could not have guessed; and all of those are now at our command, available to us, just for the asking, and for the courage to forget the old, and instead, trust in the Covenant and face the new with jubilation in our hearts."

Night Flight

It is a misty, orange hued London night.

I am walking down the street, my hands which aren't hands in the pockets of a coat which isn't a coat, and the misty cold streams into me; I breathe it in, all of it, including the many scents and strange pollutants, the atmosphere.

It is some hours past midnight, and the streets are mostly empty here; there are a few cars still, an empty brightly lit bus in the distance, and most of the houses are asleep.

I walk and make a point of making sure that my footfalls produce an echo sound, a contact sound. It amuses me for a while until I feel that I've got it right.

I could walk like this forever. I would never tire, never cease. There is a man walking in the opposite direction; he is well dressed, hurrying. I can see him on the straight pavement from the distance, and I can see his layers and his levels, all it takes is just a slight adjustment in my vision.

It is fantastic to be here, to have all these choices.

I could be a real vampire of the song and tale, enchant this man on this dark street and take him, leaving absolutely not a trace behind; I could just sneakily tap into a particularly tasty aspect and take a sip here, a sip there, snack on his better facets; I can let him be.

As we come closer, as I tune in more finely, further options come to my awareness. There are places within him that are empty, dark; I could fill these, light these. I could place a small candle or a star in the midst of these dark places and that would bring him life and new unfoldments.

There are other places, pathways, channels that are in some disarray; I could straighten these and make them flow again as they were once designed to flow and I have not a doubt that this would brighten him.

We are healers?

Ah, but this is extraordinary, exquisite.

I know and I remember that there used to be a thousand rules regarding conduct of this kind, and all of it most strictly not allowed, forbidden in the absolute. The likes of us were never to look to his kind for entertainment or for purpose; we were incestuous to the extreme and kept away from these, for so long.

A hundred millennia, maybe more?

Why?

I am slowing down in order not to have this end so soon; I want to keep watching this one, finding out about him, finding out what else I could do to him, with him, through him that I don't yet know I can.

Slow down.

I have commanded him without intent on my part, it was just a thought but it travelled straight across to this stranger in the night, and he received it and now we are both walking very slowly, still on a trajectory that will cause a meeting in the middle, should we thus continue and neither was to step aside.

Then it hits me – I can fly!

I must be able to fly.

I can shape and shift myself into any density, oh my dear Lord above!

The man is forgotten in an instant as I reach around and inside, try and find the right weight, the right state, and it's there, it is absolutely there, of course it is, they know, I know, oh dear Lord, here it is!

I laugh aloud and spread my arms, lean forward and adjust myself, think myself forward and up – and instantly, I rise, I fly, fast, very fast I swoop forward, the angle is a little too shallow and causes the man to drop to his knees, raise his arm protectively before his eyes as I rush straight over him, up and out, into the night sky.

PART 4

1: Steve Burrows

Monday, December 19th, 3 am.

John Eldrich is swooping over London and his joy and sheer delight is so noisy, we cannot ignore it any longer.

There are three fledglings here – me, Xiao Hong and John. We have been made new very recently, and I am frankly amazed and appalled yet again when I realise that only Gaius Levinius has ever taken wing in that fashion – neither Mark nor Alexandra have ever flown!

Honestly.

I can't believe their society.

It is preposterous in its stiffness, slowness, seriousness.

Here they are – well, here WE are.

We are all of this, and only God alone knows what else we can do, what else we are, and they've sat around for a hundred thousand years and what?

What did they do with any of it?

Quote rules and regulations at each other until they fell into dust?

Where is the fun in that?

And here is John. A real stiff upper lipped English gentleman, of the old school. Of the very old school, at that, the man was well beyond retirement age already and struggling to keep breathing, and here he is now, flying and literally screaming with delight and excitement through the levels and the layers.

I can sense the community waking up, all around the globe, and I bet a million people in old London town will have some very strange dreams tonight, as well.

That's it.

That is it.

I'm not sitting here for another minute.

I will myself straight into the garden, out into the night that is misty, diffuse. A Jack The Ripper night and absolutely perfect for us vampires to do a spot of real vampire flying. I note that behind me,

Xiao has arrived, full of giggles she is again, that is a girl after my own heart. Alexandra is there and Gaius too, and finally, even straight laced Mark makes his appearance.

Well, whatever.

I put my head back and wonder how you do this thing. Even as I wonder, I can already feel myself rising; now that is some experience!

I put my hand up, Superman fashion and think up and forward and really that is all it takes – at the speed of thought, I fly and travel perfectly high above the rooftops, high above the aerials and wires, and it is fantastic, absolutely amazing.

I send John my delight across the sleepy lights of London, then I feel the others are right behind me.

What a night!

What an existence!

And how beautiful does all of this appear from so high up, you can't see the dirt and the mess of tarmac, concrete, all those ugly buildings. Here, there are diamonds scattered into an ocean dark; here are strings of pearls, and silky black, reflecting smooth, the long slow worm that is the Thames out on her way to sea.

When the original excitement has abated, and has turned into a kind of reverence and gratitude, a freeing feeling and a lightness, even a compassion for all those who never know what this is like, who never will, the others once again come closer to my consciousness, to my awareness.

They too are enjoying themselves, finally having some fun with these extraordinary gifts that we all hold, and for a time, we all exchange our feelings, our experiences of this night, and I am satisfied; I look around me and there's no way I can know where our house would be from here, but I don't need to.

I simply will myself right back into the garden and there I am.

God, this is so simple. So profoundly amazing. I bet there isn't a place on Earth I cannot go, and then I start to wonder if I could travel to the moon like this – I have no body and no need for oxygen, is this possible?

I bet it is.

Morning is now not long away. There is already a hint of light in the sky, and a fine, cool breeze has sprung up. I can see the stars. I can see the stars and I wonder if I can go there too, just the same.

Are we really that free?

Free to go wherever we want?

And if we are, why haven't they?

Something nudges me, something old, strange, far away – perhaps something that once belonged to Gaius, or something older still?

There is so much to learn, so much to explore – and there is still a lot to do before the festival.

That is only now two days away.

It doesn't make much difference, of that I'm sure, and I am sure as well that time is not as it may seem for us, and that these ultra-slow procedures of brainwashing they've employed here since the dawn of time are a device to stop us from discovering more about that, just the same as all their other set ups seem so custom made to keep their wings clipped, literally, at that.

I straighten myself and feel the others circling in.

They are flying here and they are using me for a beacon to make their way back.

Fair enough.

I am not their Docem, even though especially Mark and Alexandra like to treat me as if I was, but the fact is that these guys have no idea of what to do.

Now that their rules are all gone, they wander around like prisoners who've been inside far too long, and don't remember anymore that you need an umbrella on the outside if you don't want to get wet when it starts to rain.

Even Gaius has a big streak of that remaining in him and I find it amusing that he takes me for a role model, how he watches me and my reactions with such interest but behind that, he is quite in awe of me and what I do.

I'll have to be their leader for a while, at least until they find their feet ...

We shall rest.

We shall go and take a room each, no more unions for tonight, and simply rest in each other's presence, dream together for a time and when that time is done, we all have things that need to be arranged before we can move on and take the next step.

I communicate this idea to the others even as they circle and then land around me in the garden. Everyone agrees, of course, they just love it when someone tells them what to do and they don't have to figure out all by themselves just which state they should be occupying, where, and when – well granted, there's a lot of that, and I guess it can be confusing, even overwhelming, if you don't have a grand plan in mind that holds it all together.

Let's go sleep.

Dreamtime.

2: Mark Edwards

Lights in the darkness.

My house, our house.

Each one of us, a light.

More than a light, we are fires that burn with many colours, spiralling and rising up, and stars are carried high aloft and radiance surrounds us.

It is a comfort to be here and have the faint sensation of the others near; and yet to be alone is pleasant too, relaxing.

I am not quite ready to let go and let myself drift away into unconsciousness; these times have held too much and would like to think upon this for a while.

For all these years, I never really wanted to be Docem. I never really did. I tried to make myself look forward to it, but in truth, there can only ever be one Docem – and that is my Lady Adela.

I am more relieved than I would have guessed by the strange turn of events that ended all the many futures and the certainties that I had held for all this time.

And the flight of this night was a grand affirmation of all of this, both ways.

Yes, my service to the rigid rules of the lower Covenant is truly over.

And yes, the new ways are exciting, more than that, they feel right in a way that other than my Lady, nothing ever had.

I shift down a stage with the relief of this acknowledgement, and spread a little wider, become a little more diffused, a little movement into dream.

My thoughts are slowing.

At the same time as they slow, my clarity increases, my range, and now there is a wide open space before me where I could dream of anything, of anywhere, in any way, the choice is mine.

What shall I dream?

In answer, there arises far ahead and straight ahead, a swirling that at once I recognise. It is my Lady dancing, wearing finest silk, bridal silks are streaming from her hips, from her shoulders.

It is my Lady, my one true love and there is nothing else, and nothing that could take my fascination, hold my interest, draw me heart and mind and soul all just the same; my longing for her crests and rushes from me like a fiery fountain, like a shaft of brightest light, blinding in its power, in its absolute conviction.

Yet my Lady is dancing.

Her eyes are closed, and she is weaving and swaying, tall grasses rippling under gusty winds that come and go, and she is too enmeshed within her dance to see the light.

So I call to her.

I call her name, I call her being, call her louder, then I scream and my voice bursts forward from my deepest wells and cascades out, and far and wide; it falls upon, it rains upon her and at last, she slows her dance, looks up and then her eyes begin to open wide, her emerald eyes, my Lady's eyes and now, she sees me, she awakens to me; there is resonance, and there is memory, and there inside her is that longing too for me that is as clear and bright upon this day as I have seen it, and she knows me then.

Without a moment's hesitation, without another thing that is not pure delight, she rises, rushes forward, banners flying as she comes to me in radiance and in delight – my Lady, I await you open armed, and never shall we part again.

3: Adela Bach

Not until I felt him once again did I begin to realise just how forsaken I had been without him, how immeasurable my loneliness and my bereavement.

Not until I saw him, heard him, knew him to be there did I begin to realise that not a hundred thousand years spend as a tree, a river or a lake could just begin to heal my devastation at his absence, at his lack of being by my side.

But I did see, and feel and realise; and when I did, it was as though a million chains and bonds of torture shattered in an instant, and I could only follow then with what is the only one eternal law, not just the first; there's only one, and so I flew and it was the Covenant itself that gave me wings and took me straight to him and into what I had been dying for the lack of for so long – our union, one to one, the king to the queen, two equals, equally in love, and equal in their power of devotion.

We rushed, we sparked; we burned up and exchanged each other, took each other whole and we rejected nothing, took it all and gave it all in equal measure.

When we were complete, we were complete, and different, and right, and right as we had always meant to be, as it was always meant to be.

Such joy.

Such joy.

Such joy.

4: Margaret Crawley

I am sitting on a garden bench beneath a gazebo of wild roses in full bloom.

I am wearing a white cotton dress with lace, and a white hat of elegant starched muslin, with a round, sweeping brim.

In my hands, I hold a posy of garden flowers – daisies, pinks, and blue lobelia.

The weather is perfect, all is beautiful and I am a little sad, for of course, I know I'm dreaming.

I'm a little sad that even in a dream, I can't just be here and accept this; that I should be so torn apart inside that I can't even here allow the parts of me who want such childish fantasies of gardens, dresses, flowers to have a moment where they are allowed to speak, or to enjoy themselves.

This is the perfect fantasy of an English country garden. Green carpet grass, and round informal flower borders filled to the brim with the traditional mix of lupines, hollyhocks; old fashioned pinks, monbretia and bluebells, fire lilies, all together flowering here all the same time.

Across the grass comes a man, striding towards me.

I feel now tears welling up in this my own dream, for of course I recognise Steve right away. He is wearing a tuxedo, but he's taken the jacket off and has carelessly slung it over his shoulder, rolled up the shirt sleeves, taken off the bow tie and unbuttoned the top three buttons of his shirt.

He walks easily and he is smiling, waving at me.

Oh, my, but why would my own dreams torture me so?

Why show me this which I can never have, which I don't even want, this is a childish fantasy, the kind I have rejected even when I was a child for stupid, for naïve, and just the worst kind of make belief that makes you into nothing but a fool.

This is not for me!

This was never for me. I accepted that, I thought I had, and here it is, and I am crying and I cannot stop. I drop the posy at my feet and put my hands before my eyes so I don't have to see this torturous illusion any longer, and I cry as though I could create a flood of biblical proportions, and wash all of this away, drown it, and all there would be left would be an alien, tranquil sea, without desires, grey and stately, never ending ...

Let me wake up.

I want to wake up.

Please ...

But the sunshine is warm on my arms and on my shoulders, and I can hear his footsteps on the grass, the swish of his clothes as he walks.

I can hear his voice, so ultra-real, as he says, "Margaret, Margaret, why are you crying?" and sits down next to me, I can feel the bench move to his weight, his arm and shoulder brushing me as he sits down close by my side and then he puts his arm around my shoulder.

Go away. Disappear. Make this end, this isn't fair.

This is all I ever wanted.

No, it isn't!

Yes, it is!

Oh god ...

He pulls me closer to him, pulls my head towards him, takes my hat off and lays his head into my hair, kisses my hair.

I pull away from him sharply, push him away and sit back as far as I can.

"Stop this," I tell him angrily, my voice is rough and hysterical and my face is dripping, my nose is running and I don't care anymore.

"Just stop it, go away," I say again but he remains, as real as ever, and he sighs and reaches, tries to take my hand. I pull it away sharply and move my leg as well to make the point.

"Why are you so angry at me?" he asks.

I am past caring. I'm in a nightmare, I'm desperate, and what does it matter, anyway?

"You should have loved me," I tell him.

He looks surprised.

"But I always have?" he asks, uncertain.

I shake my head. The hair that flies upon that movement isn't grey, but dark blonde, slightly curly, long. That isn't my hair. Not anymore.

"You have always made fun of me," I say, and now I'm getting a sense of relief. Perhaps this is not such a bad thing. Perhaps its good, therapeutic, to tell him the truth.

"You knew that I loved you, and you used me as it suited you. That's the truth. It was cruel of you. It was more than cruel."

He looks sincerely shocked.

"I had no idea ... you felt this way," he says, struggling with the words.

"How you can you not have?" I nearly shout it at him. "Don't lie to me. Not anymore, not here. Not here."

He turns away and plays with his jacket, moves it on the bench beside him, hangs his head. He doesn't look at me when he says, "I didn't know you were so angry about it."

I believe that. I believe that he sincerely thought he was doing me a favour by letting me be his chauffer, his maid, his aunt, his confessor, his bodyguard, his slave.

It doesn't make me any less angry, though.

"You used me. I hate you for that. And I wasn't strong enough to get away from you. I hate me for that, more than I hate you. You were an addiction that I could never beat."

I take a deep, shuddering breath and wish I had a handkerchief.

Steve looks up, then he extends his hand. It is just a hand, palm up; but I hear a rushing, see a fluttering and a white dove comes down from the stately trees that are behind the bench, lands on his hand, then it melts and turns into a white handkerchief with a lace border.

Some dream this is.

I take it from him without a word and blow my nose, repeatedly.

Steve looks beaten, crestfallen. He is sitting on the bench with his elbows on his knees and hanging his head, rubbing his hair as though he was trying to wash it.

I sigh and say, "Look, it's alright. You're a selfish son of a bitch, and I let you take advantage of me. Happens all the time. I guess there's a flaw in my character, I'm just a masochist who met their sadist. It's just ... this dream, it's ... it's doing my head in."

He looks up then and sits back on the bench. He sighs as well.

"This isn't a dream, you know," he says.

I look around the garden, get up and take a couple of steps on the grass. It feels inviting, soft, and giving. I'd like to take my shoes off. As I think it, they disappear and I'm barefoot, sinking into the grass, cool, moist.

This isn't a dream.

Then what is it?

Steve laughs tiredly and answers my unspoken thought.

"I think we might call it an alternate reality."

I sit down on the grass and touch it, comb it with my fingers.

"What have you done to me this time?"

Steve sighs and says, "I've turned you into a vampire."

I shrug. "I thought there was something wrong with you. You just don't wear tuxedos."

He laughs at that and comes over to me, stands above me and looks down.

Seriously, he says, "I think I did it to repay ... everything, you know."

I don't answer. Birds are tweeting, a sweet breeze makes the foliage applaud softly all around us.

Steve continues hesitantly, "No-one has ever loved me the way you have. I never felt that I deserved it."

I'm sure you didn't, my fair friend. I'm sure no-one does. Love isn't really about deserving.

"No," he says in response to my thoughts, "No, it isn't. That's what I've learned, what I am learning. Love is about evolution, and about preciousness."

I can't help but look up at him in pure astonishment.

I've known this man for more than ten years and I would never have believed that he would actually get to a point where he might start to understand something about himself, about people, about the world.

"So was it love that made you – do to me whatever it was you did to me?" I enquire.

He sighs again. "I'm not sure," he says, "I just hope it was love, and not guilt." He walks around and sits down beside me, facing in the same direction, towards the bench, the wild roses and the trees. "All I can say is that when I knew where I was going, I wanted you to have that too, I wanted you to come, and share this with me. Only you of all the people I've ever known. Only you, and that's the truth."

I don't know what to do with that.

I don't know what to do with him, or me, for that matter.

I am a vampire?

What does that mean?

Steve looks at me and says, "I would like to show you, if you would let me. I would like to show you the union. Then you know everything I know."

I look into his fair blue eyes and I give a small snort of laughter, then a long sigh. As though I ever had a choice, since first I laid eyes on you. You captivated me, you conquered me, good and true. I might as well submit to it, give myself up to it.

There's nothing else that I could ever do, no matter how hard I tried.

Steve holds out his hand to again and this time, I simply take it.

His hand is cool and dry, and it is as though it is vibrating minutely, oscillating fast. This sets up a tremor that pulses all through my body, and as that is happening, the country garden finally begins to fade away, becomes less and less realistic, then it melts around us, from beneath us into swirls of liquid colour which all drain away in all directions until we are alone in nowhere, him and me, and I then need to hold onto him with both hands, for I am disorientated and afraid of falling into that void that has no end, falling up, or down, or to the sides, it's falling all the way.

"Falling in love," he says and smiles, draws me to him and kisses me lightly. It is a vibrant, resonant sensation and when he draws back, I can see misty lights play about his lips, colours streaming from his mouth, and I can't help myself, I must lean forward, I must taste them, want to drink them, want to drink of him, and even as I am entirely overwhelmed by the sensations, by the flavours and the feelings there's the thought right at the back, the far back of my mind that everything has changed, that I am new, and that he did the right thing, after all.

5: Gaius Levinius

Unfoldments are happening all around. I can sense a great deal of activity in this house to which I have aligned myself, to which I have come home, it could be said.

To observe Steve Burrows and his behaviours is fascinating, sometimes perplexing. I was entirely taken by surprise when he took that woman there in front of us, and in such a preposterous way. I did not understand this at all until Alexandra explained to me that in recent times, humans had depicted theatre plays of our kind which involved neck biting and blood draining in a very formalised fashion. Steve Burrows had performed a satire on his society's understanding of our transformational processes, at the same time he had initiated just such a process.

I might have been more shocked than I was if it hadn't been for the reaction of the young Docem, Edwards. Being in the presence of his intense outrage at Burrows mocking all that he had considered to be right and holy, watching and feeling him struggle to regain any form of perspective was so intriguing that I quite forgot about my own reservations; by the time Edwards had worked it through and out and had likewise been informed of Burrow's reworking of the vampire metaphor from his day, I began to see the amusement in all of it myself.

It is true that our kind had shrouded ourselves in ritual to such a degree that aspects of the original task and purpose had become forgotten or distorted in the process.

We made transformations happen that took seconds in essence, no time at all; and in the case of the former house assay John Eldrich, it was fascinating to observe that there seemed to be no ill effects from such a rapid transition.

Indeed, there was a delight about Eldrich that was intoxicating. His enthusiasm and sheer joy at his new state of being spread through the entire house and it touched me, too.

When he discovered flight all by himself, entirely spontaneously and outside of any form of supervised or regulated situation, his emanations were such that they lit up aspects of my own being that had been so long forgotten, I would not have included these in a inventory of my own states and experiences.

Yet, on that night, I flew as well; we all did, old and young alike, and I felt something – happiness, perhaps? Gratitude? I am unsure; it has been too long.

There is another aspect of this new form of my being that is both puzzling and delightful.

These unions, richer, wilder and infinitely more passionate and more intense, these unions, they enrich me.

They make me more, for every one brings to me that which was the other; they add to me, expand my understanding of myself to a new level, or it may be more precise to say that they expand me in reality.

Eldrich is so close in all his ways to being absolutely human still, it brings my own long lost humanity back into range, back into my awareness.

I had forgotten what it was to be that way.

I had forgotten who I was, and how I used to think and feel.

I had forgotten all of that, but now, I can remember.

It is extraordinary.

My life as a man was hard, but it was also majestic in the sheer brutality of every sensory impression, in the raging events that possessed me or which caught me inside themselves. Life had me by the throat; it shook me violently, tore into my flesh, ripped my intestines, chewed my testicles in iron jaws.

Blood red and fire; burning, grating reality, overwhelming, terrifying.

How could I have forgotten all of that?

Oh, of course I know how. On that level, it is obvious – it is the Arada dream that sands all of that away over time, makes it recede into a mist, further and further away until it is nothing but a far away echo, a remnant of whispers, and even then, you cannot make out any longer if there had been any words, or screams, or bugles calling then, and by then, it doesn't matter any longer.

The truth?

Not one of us ever returns from the Arada dream.

We are all still fast asleep and our existence is a dream, nothing more; we think it is perfection for we are inside the dream.

We live within a cage, a beautiful, luxurious harem in which each one of us becomes both inmate and the guards who will prevent escape; and we will sit and tell each other tales of just how good it is to be right where we are, and shudder at the outside, which is nothing, a darkness nothing and the only place that's right and bright, is here.

Burrows tore our sleep asunder.

He woke us up.

He woke me up.

I have been dreaming for two thousand years.

I am stunned by this, perplexed.

I don't know how I should respond to this understanding, whether I should be dismayed at the loss of life this represents or if I should seek to think of it in a different way altogether.

What is this Arada dream that we enter into and then not ever leave again?

What is its purpose?

I let myself fall backwards and I drift and try to shift my point of view.

I try to formulate a question to which the only answer that can be is to make sure that my kind should go to sleep and dream and never be quite present, never be in contact with the unbelievable excitement of the wild that is the truth of not just all the universe, but of our kind just the same.

We are born here, we are the children of the wild, we belong right here and not locked up in dreams.

I seek the question, but I cannot find it; I don't understand.

All around me are unfoldments, unions taking place, explorations being conducted just the same as I am seeking to find home and hearth in all this that has never been and where there are no paths, no guidelines and no masters who would tell us what to do.

It is there, but it is unknowable. The wild is not to be mastered, it is not to be kept at bay. We are here, and we must learn its ways, must learn to tread with care and follow where the wind will take us, where the streams of time and tides of deeper, older movements guide our paths.

I look ahead and to the future.

Infinite complexity.

Patterns beyond patterns.

Shifting, drifting, swirling unfoldments.

Great spheres rising, touching, receding.

And in the midst, there is a star fire, a bright place of inordinate power and divergence that draws me irresistibly towards it.

The festival.

It is there.

And we are drifting ever closer.

6: Xiao Hong

The unbelievable event that was Mark and Adela in union pulled me out of my own sphere, out of my own center and swept me up like a leaf in a hurricane.

Round and round, upside down, inside out, back to front, I was tossed and buffeted, completely disorientated and at the same time, I knew that this was an opportunity for me.

I slowed myself, I slowed right down until the rushing, crazy movements inside and out became a dance, and then a soft and silent forward drifting, and then I simply stopped and everything was still.

Now, I could move in freedom, and I went outside of it so I could get an overview.

There they were, two galaxies colliding; indescribable, unspeakable.

But there were we, all of us, and others too, drawn to this event, swept up in the event, many others, some closer, some further away but all were touched by this and by the swirling streams and powerful tides the event created across the levels, across the layers.

And there was I.

Not a leaf but a star in my own right, a star made up of many lights and many fires, and I was beautiful.

There was a starry trail that showed my passage, showed my path as it had been, and I could see how it would then continue; there was a pattern there prescribed and as I traced it I did know it, and I recognised it for my own.

And so, I went back and inside myself, and I stepped right inside myself, extended me as though a hand was slipping right into a glove made in perfection into every part of that, flowed smoothly and luxuriously all the way, through all the rivers and the tributaries, the capillaries and out, a web, a breath of starlight; and when I had thus inhabited me in my entirety, I was connected and I knew not just the path, but also how it came to be, how my own being was directed and directing in conjunction with all else, in harmony.

Lovingly, I released my hold on time and let it move again, let my awareness come into the same movement, find the rhythm, find the rhyme and when it meshed so perfectly, I then was free to be a dancer, be a sail, be as a bird and fly the storm, be part of it, and take the storm and make it carry me to where I want to go, to where I need to be.

Ah, but this is exquisite!

The fantastic shooting stars of energies displaced, the incredible powerful discharges and waves upon waves that ripple and rush from the center of their union create bridges to places I have never been; they make connections, updrafts upon which I can ride to touch new planes, new times and new existences.

High up above and in a sphere I could never have reached without the lifting power of their union I recognise Gaius, and I make my way to him, a complex spiral path with many loops and many angles but I navigate with ease and draw alongside him in delight.

He is amazed at this contact, doesn't recognise me at first, for how could a one such as me be here? How could anyone reach him on this level?

He is used to being so alone.

Delightful, deliciously attractive – he is an undiscovered country, an unconquered territory that is awaiting my footfall and what riches might I find here?

Gaius.

I have come for you.

7: Alexandra Zyskowska

There was a time when rest meant drifting quietly, in peace and deep reflection.

There was a time when most serenely, all the members of his house would be together and we would be just like a field of stars, silent, vibrant, cool and clear.

This, here, could not be more different!

Within moments of our withdrawal and relaxation, all manner of explosions ensued, all manner of the most amazing unions, creating force fields and fountainheads, all around me, everywhere.

I was completely astonished by all of this, a chain reaction that seemed to sweep everyone somewhere and into something, no-one was left untouched by the sheer intensity of what was happening.

When my Lady Adela returned, it went through a threshold; by then, my own need for union was such that I was bouncing between levels randomly, a shooting star on an unknown trajectory, out of control and at the mercy of these energies, of these emotions, that soon enough turned into feelings, then they are like sounds; great winds that buffet me, distort my shape and try to make me into something of their choosing, a sculptor at work who is intent on making something like the world has never seen.

Far on my right, I perceive another shooting star unfoldment – it is Xiao Hong who even as I watch her, takes control and turns herself into a shape, a flying being, like an angel does she rise; she dives into these awesome tides with purpose and she soars there, swims with the currents, uses them to lift her up, and up.

As I observe her and her movements, in turn I mimic them and find that what she's doing is exactly right.

In these conditions, it is not correct to simply drift without volition and be storm tossed, here and there; it is essential that we should become an active part of these unfoldments and decide just how we want to use this time, this landscape.

It offers much opportunity, once it is understood that this is more than just a crazy chaos of disturbance, of upheaval.

I watch Xiao Hong gain speed and height, on a path, a course and as I extrapolate her trajectory, I see that she is on her way to Gaius, who exists above the rest of us; that is a good choice indeed and I wish her well on that endeavour.

I lean into the movements then and I concentrate on learning how to fly here, how to stretch and use these powerful currents to take me here, and there; and so it is that I find my potential and conversion John, fluttering helplessly in this storm and in sincere distress, about to be engulfed by great pulsating waves of forest green and midnight blue being generated by Mark and Adela as their union gathers speed and power.

Trying to fly inside these incredible fields is an amazing challenge.

There is no way I can make headway by trying to cross them or fight against them, I have to attune to their inherent ebb and flow and use these as a springboard from one occurrence to the next; and soon, I am alongside John and once again, I offer him the safety of my protection, of my existence.

I find this curiously rewarding, delightful and it makes me feel different, greater; even in these ocean storms, I am a light and I have a purpose, and I can make a difference here.

My presence is welcomed with open arms and immense relief; at first, I enfold him and lay a course for us to move up and out, higher and further away from the center of the vortex, into a clearer space where we are absolutely still a part of this and can observe and feel it all, yet there's no danger any longer to be swept into unfoldments that are strictly not of our concern, at least not yet.

I find a stability, an oasis space and there I gently let him go to find his bearings, re-establish himself and gain perspective on it all.

He resonates in gratitude and relief and I observe him, watch him looking out at the extraordinary universe that is our house in full unfoldment, trying to understand, trying to comprehend the incomprehensible.

Gently I move up behind him, lean against him, and as I do, I become aware that he is attractive, that there is a beautiful strength inside of him, an innocence and a purity which I have rarely felt like this. He is untouched, virginial; he his young and there is something about him that resonates to something within me in the strangest way. As I tune to him, more and more, the galaxies and firestorms recede; as wonderful a spectacle and an experience these things are, I am drawn to the universe that lies inside of him, inside of me.

What is this resonance, how are we the same? And then I see it, can't believe it, can't believe that I had no idea, that I didn't know.

Of course. He knows my mistress, the Lady of my first union.

He knows the Lady Catherine.

She must have been his Cestra, chose him for potential, just as she chose me to be Arada, and both of us have her inside of us, we are her children in a way, although she never was his Lady.

A deep welling of longing rises up inside of me then, a something I have carefully avoided, something I don't think about – my Lady, my first love, my only love. She came to me in hues of sunrise, gold and golden rosy purples, and she was my sunrise, my goddess, is my goddess still, oh!

Lady Catherine!

As I cry out, the other one is swept away with recognition, but he has different recollections, yet he knows that we are longing for the same one, to him, a distant, perfect dawn of promise, and to me, the sunrise manifest; Catherine as Cestra, and as Docem, and still, Catherine it is.

Catherine it is.

As we agree and show each other our perspectives and our knowings, there unfolds between us a creation that is dawn and sunrise both and in the same place, at the same time; and we weave around this, dance in drifting veils about it and it comes to me that what we're doing isn't right, that we are worshipping an illusion, an evocation, some thing that we have made and no matter what, could never be the whole truth of the matter, the whole truth of the being we once knew and held within us with such fervour and devotion.

This knowing slows my dance and I step back a little, then a little more; and here, I have now the perspective to observe just how the fascination, longing and creation makes a feedback loop that still has John entirely enthralled, keeps him locked up within itself and strengthens more and still yet more with every orbit he prescribes in flight about his non-existent star.

His focus is amazing. It is near enough complete. It has become locked on a single point that is off center and thus causes him to go in everlasting circles; it is stable and it doesn't change, will never change until eternity.

The first law of the Covenant is love.

The second is unfoldment.

The third is preciousness.

This system ignores them all.

I understand then that I have seen the preciousness in John when he was still a man; that I can't help but want for his unfoldments to be splendid; and that I love him.

When all these three come into line, and into my awareness, I change; I change as from my deepest center, a new star is born; it springs into existence with a brilliant force and power, is pure and so inordinately bright, it breaks the focus he has held for oh so long and so his flight becomes erratic, his dance becomes confusion, and finally, and finally, he turns away from that ghostly evocation he himself has made to give himself a reason to continue on at all, and then he sees me.

I am no dawn.

I am no sunrise.

I am your star.

8: John Eldrich

They call it union, but I call it making love.

Perhaps that's wrong too.

Perhaps it should be called, becoming love?

I thought I knew what love was, I thought I was in love for all these years, but I had been wrong.

There is a difference between love, and obsession.

Love heals you, whichever way you touch it.

It heals you if you give it, and just the same, if you receive it.

There is no difference.

It is beautiful, well, that word does not describe it, no word could, nothing could.

If it hurts, if it makes you sad, if it makes you tired or distraught, my friend, that isn't love.

I would have argued fiercely, desperately, when I was still clinging on to my complete illusion, born from loneliness and total lack of knowledge or of understanding.

I would have rather died than to accept that my obsession with the Lady Catherine was that – a terrible disease, something that harms and thereby, it could never have been love.

Only now I know the difference.

Alexandra showed me, taught me, and in doing so, she set me free.

And that as well is something I could never understand before.

True love does never bind you to another; it frees you in every way, it gives you wings and never would you think that you're beholden, or that there can only be the one, THAT one – love has no name, it has no face, it has no colour, no conviction and it asks you not a thing.

It demands nothing.

Now, that I finally know what it is, I am free to love.

I am free to love Alexandra, and all the others here, and all and everything – there is no hierarchy in love, no preference, no jealousy.

Love is a coin where both sides are the same – it is one and everything, alpha and omega, and it is eternal.

I left love and lived in an illusion of my own making.

I spoke its name in vain.

But even that is now just as it was, and I am free for love knows not of guilt, or shame; it overwhelms regret and sorrow, washes away all sins and replaces everything that went before with nothing but its own splendour, reflected in everything it touches, and that is every thing.

Over the years I knew of the others, I also knew that they lived by a law they called the Covenant. I even knew the rules and regulations that were part and parcel of this law they followed with a total and unquestioning loyalty that often struck me strangely; the young ones and the old ones just the same.

Now I know why.

To have experienced the living reality of love the way I did does not leave room for doubt or argument; and further still, you cannot even serve love, or dedicate yourself to such a service or a task.

You cannot make a vow to love; all that is nothing but illusion.

The Covenant is their word for the reality of love; it is a bridge or a device so that those parts who would not ever comprehend the depth and width and full eternity of what that was might have a foothold, nothing more.

I am free.

We all are.

PART 5

1: Steve Burrows

Steps In The Darkness

I am the vampire messiah.

I am the one they have awaited for so long.

I know I am.

I knew, a long time before all this had come pass; I knew deep inside that there was a purpose to my existence, an old and ancient purpose.

Where did I come from?

How did I come to be here, to be me, to be exactly what I am, and how did all my footfalls lead me to be here and now?

Was there ever a time when I could have chosen to make it different, to stop all this from happening?

I know there wasn't.

This is not my doing, and none of this is my choice.

I am an instrument.

I am a catalyst.

I have a task and I have a purpose, long planned, long devised, and I don't know what it is.

I can't see that far ahead.

I am on a path that is dark to me in all directions.

Where I place my foot, the next part of the path arises in return; and this is how its always been, and nothing I could ever do could make the slightest change.

I tried to kill myself a dozen times or more, before that night came and I was commanded to attend the exhibition.

I took pills and overdoses; I tried to hang myself. I opened my veins in a warm bath like the old Romans did; that was romantic but once again, by a sheer fluke of luck or tragedy, I was found in time.

Once, I jumped off a motorway bridge.

I broke my legs, my hips, my shoulder. I caused a massive pile up in which five innocent people died. But I lived again, healed perfectly again.

That's when I gave it up for a lost cause.

Someone, something wanted me to live, but I could never figure out why.

What was my purpose?

I still don't know the answer to that question, but now I know that I'll find out, if I keep taking just that single step into the darkness, one at a time.

Over time, that makes a trail that leads from A to B, perhaps to Z, from alpha to omega even.

Some things I know.

I know that I have to take my new house of vampires wild to the Festival of Blessings. I know that much.

I know that there is still more preparation, that we have to go into the Underworld, what a fun term that is, indeed, and wake the sleeping Arada there.

I know that the Arada are exactly placed to be the perfect compliment and power source for this my house; that just as many years ago as it had taken, very specifically selected individuals were chosen and put here so that they would be here, right now.

All through this thing, there had been always a sense of recognition.

When I met Adela Bach, I already knew her; when I met Edwards, the sense of being involved in an ancient play that had been running to exhaustion was already there, for him as well as was for me.

Gaius and Margaret, from the opposing ends of the scale, they could be no-one else, and all of this is like a totally inevitable – well, I might as well use that term for I don't know what else to call it – this is a totally inevitable unfoldment, just like a river must run down the hills and through the valleys so that it may join the sea, become an ocean.

I am calm within.

Sometimes, a trace of wonder or surprise, appalment, insecurity, fear, indecision sweeps along, much like a piece of wrapping paper blows down a street; it is entirely of no concern and one might wonder for the briefest moment where it will eventually go, where it will end up but then it is gone from view and ceases to exist.

There is a certain security in knowing that I don't know what I'm doing, but at the same time, I can't do it wrong.

I've accepted that and now, I just move the events or perhaps, the events move me, or perhaps, I am an event that has its place and that is that, when all is said and done.

I watch and listen with detached interest as all the members of my house engage within themselves, within each other and learn the things that they must learn, change into who they must be when time has come.

There is in truth just one more thing now left to do.

I wait with patience and observe as they all find each other, go through their unfoldments as they must and settle down in their new states of being, in their new positions, most specific for each one; they might not know this yet for sure but we are a machine, a living organism where each aspect needs to be in correct correlation and functioning as one.

As yet, the bigger picture can't be seen; for that, we need the six Arada who are dreaming still and getting ready for us, just as we are getting ready to embrace them, add their fuel to our machine.

Before we do this, I need to address the others, stabilise the system, draw us together, and then, we can take the next step into the darkness.

Halls Of Marble

I have called the house together in a special place.

On the plane of existence where I first met with Mark Edwards and with Xiao Hong, I have constructed a meeting place.

I went there, where the blue endless sky lies above an endless sweep of greenest valley, and the building grew from the structure of the land; a white temple building, perfect proportions, the ancient mother and father to the temples of the ages.

I know this building well.

I've dreamed of it, I've walked amidst the halls of marble and of ice; and I wondered what its purpose was.

As I watch it become and shape itself into existence, I know the purpose.

This is our house.

It is a massive structure, built for giants; and of course, we are, we are much more and so much larger than we think, still bound to memories of bodies and of human dimensions as we are.

I smile and think of Eldrich, growing his appearance so he could fit his suit.

This building serves a purpose similar to this.

In order to inhabit it, we shall have to grow in every way.

In order to inhabit it, and to use it.

For now, I shall simply call a meeting.

Round Table

At the heart of the marble halls lies a circular room, vast and entirely without decoration. In the center stands a round and sweeping construction, more of a balcony that a table as such, which allows for many to stand in a circle, place their hands on the railing and become a part of a conductor that involves not just the building and the plane from which it has arisen, but a great deal more beside.

The central space is empty and great; there is room for things to manifest, to be observed, for portals to open – I see so many things, I'm not sure if I remember these things or if I am picking up on information that is resident right here.

It matters little, I guess.

There are no chairs here, and the circular sweep of the white marble railing shows no positional preference.

This is a true round table, without hierarchy, for equals to come together and to make things happen, dramatic things, wonderful things, miraculous things.

I walk to the table, step up and place my hands upon the cool white marble. It immediately begins to draw on me, conduct me and at the same instance, feeds me back upon myself, both directions at the same time, a surprising and pleasant sensation.

If I stood here for long enough, all by myself, I'm sure I'd learn many things about me in this way.

But that is not why I am here.

I look up to the ceiling, high, sweeping arched dome rising above the round table.

Here, I know I can see anything I choose; for now, I choose to see my house, and that is not the building there in London on a different plane and then it was, but my companions who have settled down into their new and different states of being and who are awaiting just this call.

They are a system already, strong, bound by many strands of all their interactions. You can see it taking shape and you can see the same that it is not yet finished; has not yet reached a new potential that will break a threshold and it will become a different entity entirely.

Yet even that is already here; prescribed in whispers of a future yet to come, or of a past that once had been; in this place, it is difficult to tell the difference, or perhaps there is no difference, when all is said and done.

I reach to them, I call them and I set a pulsing note to guide them here.

One by one, they break formation and they fly towards my guiding star, elegant swooping and soaring each and every one; beautiful they are, bright, alert and ready, each one a powerhouse of many different things, and as they swarm towards me I am filled with pride, and with delight, and then, with nothing but my love and admiration for their pure existence and all their many states of being.

One by one, they break through the roof of the building, come from the stars, shiny light creatures with wings, beautiful ephemeral dragons, and their shape is shifting as they come to land in their positions at the table, they shift and grow to the dimensions of the halls and manifest, one at a time.

Gaius Levinius is first, followed by Mark Edwards and Adela Bach.

Alexandra arrives, Xiao Hong, John Eldrich. I unfold Margaret Crawley from within me so she too may take her place her and she flutters into being on my right.

Each one stands, and each one rises to the new occasion, this new environment that does demand a certain shape, invites a certain state of being, and as we grow, and then begin to glow and lose some aspects of our human states and in return, gain others that we held but never thought to show, eight angels have arrived within the marble hall and now, they place their hands and wings upon the circular conductor, making us as one.

This is union of unknown power, multi-fold dimensions.

We rush into and through each other.

Aspects are dislodged and carried; systems find new components and give up others in return; the flow is a continuum that seeks to find its level, its perfect balance throughout and therefore by needs it changes us to its own preferences, clears us up, removes some things that don't belong with us and brings us new information, food, connectors, parts of bridges, a fascinating process that begins to slow as less and less is needed to be done, and finally, we resonate in absolute perfection and in perfect harmony, and the stream simply passes through each one, connects us, yet we are a group of clearly defined individuals who share a common goal, and nothing more.

I extend a welcome to us all and I receive all of our smiles and welcomes in return, including my own.

We are in deep alignment and in harmony.

Arada Diamond

We shimmer into existence in the old house in London, in the formal reception room where there is plenty of floor space for us to keep our respective formation upon arrival.

I take a moment to adjust myself and look around the circle.

I have to smile at us.

Each one of us presents in a specific way, and it seems, there have been changes.

I am still wearing a tuxedo, but it is white – to any unwary human, I must look like a 1980s pop star and I find it amusing that I should have brought this angelic existence thing, this saviour thing, into this reality in such a crass metaphor. But why not? There is no merit in being coy, or second guessing myself; so I'm wearing a white tuxedo today.

So what.

I could be wearing women's clothes, and a woman's body if I wanted to, it makes no difference, really, it doesn't.

Lady Adela comes dressed in a flowing gown of green and pink shimmering silk and Edwards looks like a 19th century bridegroom in an old fashioned suit of subtle grey with a high collared ruffled shirt and matching grey silk necktie. He looks older, there is even a touch of silver over his ears. It suits him, it is more congruent than that Peter Pan look he used to hold.

John Eldrich is hardly recognisable. He looks very young, boyish, charming; and Alexandra too seems to have lost a few years since her last manifestation.

Xiao Hong, on the other hand, seems to have gained at least a couple of decades and comes in full glow of an amazing mature woman, in oriental luscious red, gold and green. Gaius is younger than he was, more physical, more present, and Margaret ...

I look at her and have to give her a small bow. The amazing thing is that she doesn't look that much different from how she did before, and yet she appears entirely transformed, with poise and clarity, radiance and strength, a cool beauty that is immensely attractive in her understated suit of dove grey that accentuates her eyes and skin.

We are an interesting group, to be sure, and should I have seen us at a party or a gathering of any kind, I would have been most intrigued and might have tried to sneak my way into this circle.

We are present, and correct, and now it is time to awaken the Arada.

I am quite excited by the notion; the group is excited and that puts a double vibrancy into the atmosphere, into this time space.

As one, we turn and the nearest to the door leads the way out and into the corridor, to the bright mirror that is the doorway to the Underworld.

Gaius phases through the mirror, and we follow, one after the other.

I am the last to pass through and begin the descent down the spiral stairs into the womb of this house.

The Arada are aware of us.

They lie so still and pale, their bodies are already thin and fragile but their other bodies have grown strong and they fill in the gaps.

The sense of excitement that we are bringing to this occasion is mirrored by the Arada and adds a third dimension; now excitement is all around and everywhere, and I become aware that I am trembling.

There are six Arada, and there are eight of us.

How are we going to do this?

Should there be some kind of ceremony, a speech perhaps?

We're all standing at the foot of the stairs in a group and looking across the empty floor space to the center where the altars of the Arada support them gently and lovingly.

The room is resonant and filled with dreams, with thoughts, and with desire; with energies of all kinds, with vibrations; ours and theirs, and back to when there were others here, other sleepers, other feeders, other caretakers for they too left a part of themselves behind, imprints of their existence, like initials carved into a desk.

I feel the others are waiting for me, waiting for my decision, for my next move but I'm unsure.

It is true that as I see their colours and their vibrant webs, I can feel the now familiar hunger building up, a hunger that is not for food and feeding, but for union, to be sure; but each is a treasure, each one is unique, and I can't choose a one amongst them.

I want them all, and equally.

I step back slightly from the situation to give me room to think, to seek for guidance, and I notice that the others feel the same way as I do; they too can't seem to make a choice.

And then I know and I remember what to do.

We all took John together; it was a starburst union, five to one, a fantastic celebration of his birth into this new part of his life, immensely satisfying and complete; this is a similar situation and of course, we just had practice in the halls of marble how to be together, and as one.

As I know, everyone knows; and as though we were one body, all of us begin to walk and we take our places then; one of us to one Arada, apart from Gaius and I.

Here now, we shift and as we do, Gaius takes the lower dimension whilst I rise up so that we form a double six sided pyramid, a fantastic diamond shape between us which holds the Arada within.

Inside this field, the Arada begin to awaken, charged they are by the pure and powerful energies that our beings channel from node to node; they begin to awaken, but they also begin to draw together, and this is as it should be, for they will make a union first amongst themselves, and then what they are, and what we are, will combine, pass in and through and out of one another, thus making this great union then complete.

I am amazed that I know exactly what this is, that I know what to do and that Gaius and I hold this whole field steady at the poles; we are bright stars of immense power and we both direct and stabilise the entire unfoldment, this entire grid.

In unison, we begin to step up the flow of energy through our system; we speed it up, make it faster, stronger, and that pushes the Arada in the center closer towards union; faster, faster still and then they catalyse – a wondrous implosion, then a fountain birth of utter brilliance that rushes into all dimensions but is encapsulated and embraced by our field, then channelled into it – as they come home to us, as they join us, it is a brightwhite wave that leaves no consciousness behind of any kind, and makes us all be one, and many.

2: John Eldrich

Party

It is night over London, once again.

This is the last night, or maybe the first; who is to know?

Sixty years have passed since I last made my way to the theatre.

A lot has happened since then.

I was always alone, but that is no longer so.

I am now a part of a group that is quite other than I could have ever expected.

We came back from the union and re-established in the drawing room; and everyone was absolutely aware that we were assuming these shapes, these ideas of who or what we might be, most possibly for the last time, ever.

It was the strangest thing.

We got dressed for the festival.

We looked at each other, talked with each other, just like humans do. We laughed and joked, tried different transformations, different appearances; there was a small undercurrent of sadness there as fourteen vampires who between them must have been millennia old played at dressing up at the old London house.

I would imagine that this game we played there was not just a way to pass the time before we finally could leave and start out on our way to our unknown futures, or unfoldments as they should be called. I think it was a way to make a binding on a different level altogether, to have us recognise each other in that human way, to learn each others names and look upon each other with a setting that precludes so many layers and so many levels, tells the story in a different way, with metaphors of clothes and skin and hair, with movements, sounds of voices, ways of laughing, turning, walking.

This game is the last for the human child within; and although it is a game, we are getting dressed up for real, and we are on our way to a real party, where the grown ups are, and where we will cause chaos, and a revolution.

I explained to Margaret in words as we stood and talked, and felt comfortable and familiar with each other as we are the youngest here by far.

"Their society was always – and still is, everywhere but here – ruled by a system of ascencion, casts of time and experience you might call them," I told her. "The festival is absolutely organised according to these definitions, there is a place for everyone and everyone there has their place.

"The festival is a machine that has run in the same way for a hundred thousand years, and tonight, we will blow this machine apart, and something else will have to come, arise where the machine had been, and no-one knows what that will be."

Margaret nods seriously. She knows these things but just like it helps me explain it to her in the old familiar way, I know it helps her to hear words, and to be able to think, ask questions and respond.

She strokes her hair, but her hand goes straight through it and into her head; she laughs, shakes her head in consternation. Her eyebrows furrow and she tries again; this time, her hand strokes her hair backwards quite perfectly.

We smile at each other and she asks, "Do you think there will be trouble? Will they try and stop us? Can they hurt us?"

I don't know the answer to that question. What we are about to do has never been done before, it has never even been attempted. Who is to know how these other vampires will react? No-one here knows; and further, the oldest here is Gaius and he was only Segar before he laid that down and became one of us instead. No-one here has any idea of what the others might be like, or how they think; there are the Cardor, the Essem and what about the Taray, the whispering elders?

The train of thought has disturbed me and this noticed by everyone of course; yet it is Mark Edwards who comes over to us both. He looks relaxed, charming and as though he was the host of this strange party; a cigar would go nicely with his stance and states of being.

He laughs at this my thought, then says carefully, "What we all need to do is to hold clearly to the Covenant. This is an unfoldment, absolutely. It can't be anything else. Being an unfoldment, it is protected by the Covenant, and no-one will transgress against that, least of all the Cardor, who are the dedicated servants of the Covenant.

"They may even co-operate with us. Who is to know?"

Margaret and I are not really soothed by his speech so he laughs and takes us both by the shoulder and says, "Don't worry. Don't think too much. It would be a shame to spoil this night. We are together, we are in the right time and at the right place, and all is proceeding with inevitability. Soon enough, we shall also know exactly what did happen on the night."

We smile in return, he leaves us and makes back towards his Lady Adela, who is reclining by the fire place, looking as splendid as a Norse goddess might and who is clearly and deeply in love, at the very most personal level.

I don't want to think in that direction, don't even want to think about the fact that Catherine might well be there tonight, for that would spin me out and far away from where I want to be, so I put my focus on Margaret with some force of will.

"You know, it is fantastic," I say to her. "I hope you get to see it as it was, at least for a little while. The Festival is the event of a lifetime, and that's a fact, and no matter how many lifetimes you might want to count that in."

Margaret, who has been seeking to find Steve Burrows amidst the shifting groups of people in the room, turns back to me.

"Tell me about it," she says. "Just talk to me. If you would, John ..."

I understand her perfectly and it is good to talk. I have always wanted to tell someone about my festival, and I never could. That in and of itself is extraordinary, and I wonder if this gathering is exactly what this kind of thing is about – to tidy up some essential loose ends that can only be tidied right here, and never again afterwards, no matter how high we might be flying, or what kind of gods we may become.

"The music is ... otherworldly," I begin slowly. "At the time, I thought there were musicians playing these unheard of instruments, I also thought I saw them. But then, later, after learning things from Gaius and from Mark, I think I know now there are no musicians at all, no musical instruments. It is ..." I stop, because I don't want to use the word, a mind game.

It isn't that, and it really isn't. It is far more, deeper, richer.

"It is the vampires singing. Not one or two, but all of them sing together, sing softly, that's the music we potentials hear, that is what makes us dance."

I want to sigh.

"You can sigh," says Margaret gently, kindly. "You can breathe. It is comforting to do it, even though it is illusionary."

I look at her and I am sincerely grateful for her presence, for her poise. She has taken this whole thing in her stride much better than I have. She is precious, and yes, I love her.

And then I start to breathe, breathe deeply, rhythmically, in and out, and Margaret matches my breath, and she is right, it comforting, more than comforting – it is pleasurable and to remember to keep the rhythm makes all these other thoughts just disappear. The lights seem slightly brighter, the colours more pronounced, the room more stable, more familiar, far more resonant.

So we keep breathing, and we stay together until Steve and Gaius who seem to be our time and space keepers make the statement that it's time to go.

Fully dressed and fully manifest, and in our case, even breathing, we begin to file from the room, through the doors and from the house, out into the street.

I make an adjustment and my illusionary breath becomes visible, misty steam; the others laugh and copy what I did, and now we start on our way into the night, the longest night, with footfalls, with voices, with swishing clothes, with shadows and with steaming laughter breath, a party on their way to theatre.

It is Wednesday, December 21st, 7.30 pm precisely.

242

Claim

So we walk.

We walk in the night air.

The night is calm, cold, dry and bright with stars.

There is the city.

We walk just like anyone else on this night and every step is a step into the future.

It always is, and it always was.

How strange that I should never have appreciated the truth of this until right here, and now.

We don't talk.

We are aware of each other, but here, on this strange journey we have chosen to take in this way, we are people in a way. We are individuals, and each of us has their own path, even though we walk on the same pavements, stop to wait for traffic lights, then cross the road to the other side to continue on.

Past rush hour, the traffic is still extremely heavy.

Bright, blinding lights, shops, people stream in the opposite direction, and we walk amongst them, walk by them, each step a footfall into the future that becomes the past as soon as the contact is made, and the next step after that opens the door to yet another unfoldment.

So it is, so it goes.

Voices. Sirens. Engines. Music drifting. Behind that, the hum of the city, and behind that, the hum of the world.

It is the same road I walked down so many years ago, it is the same even though the buildings have changed, the signs have changed; still, it is the same road.

As then, so on this night I begin to become aware of the others who are walking towards a place where our futures intertwine; they can never meet for in time and space there is only room for a single one, no matter how hard we try to forget this and ignore this simple fact.

We all become aware of the many potentials who are on their way to the theatre.

They stand out in dress and attitude, even if an unknowing observer was to study this street with a camera placed high above; even without awareness of that shine of otherness that suffuses the potentials, each and every one, there is a similarity about them all, a group mind in action.

There are others here as well, tourists, locals who have noticed our congregation and they stop and stare at all these people who are making their way to the theatre; a small, old-fashioned theatre, so it seems, in a back road off the beaten track and yet there are hundreds of people streaming towards this, and a slow group is surrounding the double door entrance, where two stout men in dark suits with their hands clasped behind their backs stand a silent guard.

We simply fall in step with the movement of the potentials.

I am forward pointed, half in the past, half in the future and a third half of me is aware of this present; I sense Margaret close by, she is nervous and wishing that Steve Burrows would take her by the hand.

I check for him and find him likewise seeking comfort in familiarity; he is shadowing Mark Edwards. I take a moment then to scan for everyone who is in our group, and everyone is forward pointing, just the same as I was and will be again, but there is something here that makes me want to take the view, photograph in my mind their faces as they look up at the entrance steps, the gathered crowd of potentials and are in so many times all at the same time as they are right here.

It is extraordinary.

It is otherworldly.

This is not as it had been when I was here and utterly convinced that inside, my Lady Catherine was waiting.

The thought draws me into a tunnel of then and now, and both align – inside, this time, my Lady Catherine might well be waiting.

Where else would she be?

And this time, I am not a star struck potential any longer.

244

It matters not if she is a Docem now – I shall recognise her, and I shall make myself known to her, and I shall on this night of nights finally put the time to rights, and claim my union.

There.

I have thought it.

I have decided it, and thus, I've made it real, and now.

And now, there is no-one else.

There is the theatre, and the festival below.

I shall enter it entirely.

PART 6

1: Valia

The Strangeness

The more I realise myself, the more disconcerted I become.

What is this?

Is there something wrong with me?

I feel all wrong, all displaced, I feel –

"Meruvian?"

He is there, close by, my radiant beloved, and for a moment, I am relieved until I notice that the strange vibrations are a part of him as well.

This frightens me.

"Meruvian?" I call to him again, and I begin to feel a panic enveloping me. Has it finally happened? Has my time come? Have I lost the battle, am I slipping away into insanity?

I don't recognise this!

I should recognise this!

I have been here so many thousand times and it has always been the same ...

"My Lady," Meruvian unfolds more strongly, reaches to me, offers his support. "It isn't you. It is the Festival. It is different this year, something has happened."

The Festival is different?

But that is – insane!

How can that be?

I am sure that I'm insane.

Possibly I am just dreaming Meruvian and his responses; he might not be here at all, he might not be real, and none of this might be, and I wouldn't know and perhaps I'm already gone and I'm not here at all, I am a whispering ...

Strongly and powerfully, Meruvian flares through my disturbances and terrifying spirals, burns through me like a forest fire, brilliant bright and uncompromising.

"Valia," he says and sends with urgency, "Valia, it is not you. We are here at the festival. We are here, this is it – this is now, and there is something wrong. It came from the house of Adela Bach."

Adela? I remember Adela. Oh but she was beautiful! She shone like the sun over spring fields, was like the rain on autumn fields, so pure and so delightful ... Adela, my beloved child, my daughter, my lover, how long has it been since I remembered you?

I was Segar at the time, and I saw her and I fell in love with her. I saw her in a town by a river; it was a spring morning and she was walking to market with her servant girls. Where she stepped, the ground laid out a carpet of flowers for her and where she had gone, she left a scent of life and wonderment that lingered like perfume.

I found a Cestra from a house nearby and made them dream their way to her; of course, he was immediately enchanted and of course, he picked her for conversion on the spot. I watched them both the entire summer long, flowed with brooks by which they sat, rustled in the leaves of trees beneath which they sheltered, and then the winter came, and the festival, and by then, Adela knew me just as much as she would recognise the wind, the moon, the stars.

What a beautiful union, what a beautiful Arada she became ...

"My Lady ..." Meruvian embraces me gently, draws me back and down, and I am confused again. Adela? Meruvian ...

The festival.

The strangeness.

Yes, I remember now. What did he say? What was he trying to tell me?

"The strangeness ... it came from the house of Adela? What happened? How can that be?"

Even as I ask it, there is another memory, far away and up above, a Cardor memory, oh, but they are difficult, diffuse and they just don't fit into anything or anywhere. The Cardor were meeting ... I remember hearing their call ...

250

Meruvian is very concerned about me now, and this ripples into me. He isn't sure how to hold me, and he is afraid that I will leave him.

Ah, but these older days!

Sadness there is, grief.

Love, so much love for him, for me, for everyone and everything.

I can't hold it all together. I really cannot – I am everywhere and there is too much of me. My beloved, beloved ... I am so sorry. I don't want to break your heart, don't want to tear your soul apart with my leaving. I really don't and I would do anything to spare you that, to return myself to a stable state and be for you what you need me to be.

But still, and even here, my love for him renews my strength and for time, it will hold again, a shadow alliance of all these many times and places that are me but that are desperate to break apart, to drift apart and set me free.

I focus on him then, call to love that exists in all those islands of me, ask it to unify, one more time, just this one more time, hold me together, let me be here for him, this one last festival, make it so.

And so it does, and so it is – it gathers from everywhere, from everywhen, and it sets up a web above the singular alliances that provides a structure, a form for me to hold and have, and finally, clarity returns to me.

Here and now, we are at the festival.

Something is wrong, the atmosphere is all wrong.

There is a sharp expectation, a bright awareness, a coiled waiting with many undertones that exists in the community and reflects back upon itself, like swords drawn will reflect each other just before commencement of the battle.

The potentials are nervous and unsure; many are looking around, up at the stands and that is not how it has always been.

The music is missing.

Why aren't we singing?

A rushing to my right takes my attention and Meruvian and I turn to see the arrival of another Essem, Andelestra.

Strangely, his presence further strengthens me, comforts me and seems to support the structure I have build to keep myself together; and then, as more of our kind arrive, this resonates more strongly still.

Meruvian is relieved by that, deeply relieved; so much so that he is leaning to me, taking comfort from me being steady and strong like this, as though he was taking the opportunity to rest before the next onslaught of storm will drain his strength again.

As I hold him and enfold him for a change, I begin to reach and stretch into the unfoldments here, try and trace the sources of disturbance, of otherness – as soon as I do this, I find it.

The source of the disturbance is unmissable.

It is located in the stairwell and moving down towards us.

It is made up of many, and those many are made up of much; but these many are together and of one mind at the higher levels – no, wait.

I sharpen my focus, expand higher.

What I find, astonishes me.

I call to Meruvian to follow my trace and he does; the other Essem here have heard me too and all follow, a swooping flock of powerful birds or dragons rising, powerful lifting of beating wings.

We are Essem.

We are the ones of high, we are the ones who can fly the highest, see the most for we have known the most and we have mapped so many places, states of being; so much more than anyone in our community, that makes us more, and in the end, makes us too much to hold it all together.

And yet what I have seen is absolutely new.

It is a mystery.

Far higher than I have ever been there is a source of existence.

It is so impossibly high that I would not know how to reach there, and the only reason I can even perceive that there is such a high is because the many who are causing the disturbance are clearly radiating down from this much higher level, and they are beams of light that shine through clouds and touch the realms of which I know, yet they themselves originate not in the clouds, but way beyond.

Way beyond.

All of us are astonished, mystified, unravelled and appalled.

All of us Essem once were Cardor, and so we know the mysteries of the Covenant; or so we thought, for even though the Covent does speak of realms beyond the realms, it clearly states that these are not for our kind, and that we cannot find an entrance there.

But someone has, and those someones are here tonight.

They are walking down the stairs, shoulder to shoulder with the potentials of this year's festival, arriving here as the first, the newest, the youngest; arriving here as though they sought first union with our kind.

And then it shudders through me in all ways, all levels and all layers – this is the time of change.

It must be.

Tonight, right here, the oldest prophecies of the Covenant are coming to pass.

It was foretold that one would come to take us home, to set us free.

They are coming.

They are really coming.

As one, we Essem embrace the thought, the concept, and the understanding; the Cardor shifting in the stands below us feel and hear the resonance enough so that they understand and they then too pick up the call; in turn, the few Ferata who have come translate it down to Docem, they in turn now tell their Cestra and when even the Arada who are here in their dreams have heard and understood, a circuit is completed and the entire theatre resonates with it – they are coming.

It is the night of changes.

Welcome

When I was oh, so young, I was told of the night of changes, and of the one who would take us home. When I grew up and into all the stages and the structures, I forgot about it; I was reminded though when each and every festival would come; I was reminded when I was Cestra and searched for potentials, entirely oblivious of the guiding hand of Segar, Essem, sometimes of Ferata who would draw my path towards a human of their choice and their desire.

When I was Segar, I often thought about it; when I was Cardor, I was brought close up with all the ancient prophecies and I learned that they were never ancient, never old, but they existed in a timeless space where all was now, no yesterdays and no tomorrows there, the home of our Covenant.

And still, and through it all, I never thought that it would come, or that I would be there when it would come.

Much less that I would be the oldest of the Essem, and if there had been a prophecy that had foretold that I would be so radiant and so strong, so clear and finely structured, so together at that time, I might have laughed and swirled, backwards and down, for that could never be.

And yet it is, and here it is.

There is a waiting, a stillness; this is wrong, and a smile rises within me for I know just what to do, it is natural and right – here, we come and we sing together; it was always the same song, as the festival was always the same, only the players might change, flow through the system over time as water flows over a rock, and it is always new water, and yet, water nonetheless.

I raise my voice, and in the stillness, I begin to sing a new song.

It is a song of welcome, of acceptance; it is a song about the Covenant, about my life and my waiting, about my loves.

It is a different song from that which used to be; it is brighter, it is lighter and it is far more complex, with ranges that not everyone can hear, but all can hear the pulse right at the heart of this my song, and a sigh travels throughout the theatre as at first, a single second voice joins with mine in a perfect harmony – Meruvian sings with me, a perfect foil to me, and filling in dimensions that are his own, that I could never reach.

Slowly and reverently, the other Essem start to sing with us, and then it ripples down and through as every single one of us finds their voice, and their place to add their story, add their own uniqueness, their preciousness and their existence.

The potentials are bathed in this song of welcome of the new; they close their eyes and they begin to dance; but this dance too is new and such as it has never been before, and so the potentials bring their own uniqueness to this night of changes and with the movement of their bodies, they add their welcome in their own particular way, on their own level.

Ah, but it is beautiful.

So it is that when the ones who are at the center of the change step into the theatre, they are welcomed by us all.

2: Steve Burrows

They could feel us coming.

I could feel them feel us coming.

At first, there was an awareness of our presence that began to rise and spread in ripples; there was confusion, fear even, rejection of the otherness we were bringing to this festival occasion.

There was a part of me that was rather sad, because as we descended with the new potentials, I was well aware that this was not how the others remembered their festival; I had their matrix inscriptions to compare the now to then, and so it was that I would never know what it might have been like.

What it might have been like to be just a potential, excited and scared half to death, scared that I might not find Edwards here, might not see him again, that I might be rejected and would have to leave all of this, and live then, knowing of these things yet never being able to step into it, to embrace it.

I would never know that, nor would I know the dance; there would be no first union, no Arada dream.

Well, that is all of the past now. All that is behind us, and I let the thoughts drift away and leave them behind as well, a trailing wake of might have beens and nevermores, that drift apart soon enough with me as that which holds it all together moving forward, going on, being gone from there.

My house is steady, a unit, even though each one of us is thinking their own thoughts, leaving their own stream of moments behind, like snakes that shed their skin as they move forward, so we glide downwards, slow spiral stairs, deep and dark.

Beneath us and below us, they are waiting.

And now that I am here, I am not afraid.

The others below begin to shift and organise themselves; there is a guiding hand at work, one individual, greater and stronger than all the others, different from all the others, wider reaching. This one begins to resonate the basics of a harmony, this one draws all to stillness, and then there is a shift through and out into a different territory – a wide open space into which we may flow now, and I realise that they are welcoming us.

We are the arrow, they are the target, but this target is drawing the arrow towards it, inviting it to come, encouraging the forward movement and doubling the velocity – a familiar feeling, a disconcertingly familiar feeling but then we recognise it and a cry goes up amongst us – this is a union!

I am so overwhelmed by that realisation that my forward momentum nearly falters, but by now, the attraction from the others below has become a strong tide that pulls me on, nonetheless, and keeps me right on track, even though for just a moment, my own will had quite gone.

The welcoming that is awaiting us is gaining power, strength and many voices; they are singing to us.

They are as potentials, telling us of themselves, of their times and their existence, and all my house shivers through and through as we continue to move forward, at the same speed as before, but with an ever stronger gathering conviction, with an ever strengthening purpose, and an ever widening field of view, and of influence.

I begin to understand and as I do, so do the others of my house.

We open up and we begin to rise into our true selves, for here, there is a limitless amount of energy that comes straight from beyond, and it is this the ones below are seeking and requesting – they want the white light, that is what they have missed and hungered for, what they have sought and tried to find for a hundred thousand years or more, that ultimate dimension that will complete their circuitry, as it has completed ours.

It is extraordinary.

They are all potentials, awaiting transformation.

And they have waited oh! so long!

But we are here.

We are here, and they are here, and also, all these humans – we are one system, all together, we will all engage in union, and from us, there will arise something altogether new and different.

258

It is awesome.

As I rise, before me lies the times past, and I can see – everything.

I enter the theatre.

3: Valia

At the centre of the glowing star that is the many, there is the one.

High above it all, on my slow wings of stars spread out awide, I recognise the one, I see the one, and I greet the one.

An amusement ripples through me briefly.

All those millennia I have spent in many incarnations wondering if I would recognise the one if they appeared – my wondering was that of an unknowing child, for here he is, and there is not a doubt, as there could never be.

The song has stilled to silence with his arrival.

All is silent now.

All is reverent, holy.

Time stands still in adoration, in celebration of this wonderful event, this moment of becoming, and here is all the time and space there ever was, there ever could have been, an infinity awaiting our footfalls.

On one level, we are all assembled here.

Rise above it, and there are less, and less.

Go to the furthest point, and the theatre is entirely empty, and there is only the one, standing in the centre, standing tall, alone.

He is the future, and I am the past.

We belong together, for it is in our union that the now arises, that reality becomes and time grows, a slow rose unfolding, our child conceived.

From the stars, I assemble my crown of light.

With exquisite tenderness, I shape myself and lay the cloak of the Covenant about my shoulders.

I call to me – all.

And all comes streaming to me, all the levels and layers, all that has been, everything. I am a hundred thousand years, I am a million of my kind, I am the days and nights and all sensations, every thought, each dance, each movement and the tears of joy and sadness too.

I am all of that, a living repository, an hourglass that is receiving all the grains of sand now in the final moments, and I take it all, enfold it to me, have it come home to me, have it fill me and raise to overflowing – I am a fountain, ancient, pure, of light and life, lives then and lives remembered, so many visions, so many colours, so many souls.

And I take it all to him.

I take myself to him.

I take myself to him, the one, and before him, I bow deeply and I spread my arms awide and offer everything to him.

He takes my hand and raises me, bids me to stand, for we are equals.

His eyes are all the days to come, all the stars not yet to be; infinity, so dark and vibrant with potentiality, and hungry, ready to receive what I have brought to him.

Around us, far away, there is a chorus softly singing, far away.

I recognise the voices, know that here, there are the elders; they have waited for this moment, waited here to weave a shroud for us so we may dance, so we may now begin to gently and so sweetly lean towards each other, sense our way towards a movement, to a resolution that will take us through and out, our union and a dance that will change the universe forever.

And here, high up and far away our dance begins; and as we gently weave and go into the spiral movements of enfolding one into the other, our dance traverses down and down, encompassing the levels and the layers, and drawing all and everyone into its wake – we dance the dance of life and so, it is complete.

EPILOGUE

John Eldrich: The Seeds

They said there was an ancient prophecy.

The ancient prophecy foretold that one would come who would set them free and take them home.

I don't think that anyone other than perhaps the likes of us from the last days of transition, a hundred thousand years ago or maybe more, really took that seriously, or understood that it was entirely literal.

One did come.

He did set them all free from their strange timeless dream existence that was never either quite here, or there.

And I think he did take them home.

In the theatre, Steve left us and made for the central floor space. The potentials moved out of his way, and there was such silence that you could hear a pin drop.

He stood there alone, until a Lady came to him, a Lady of stars.

They danced and caused a whirlpool that eventually picked up everyone and everything around them yet it left us untouched and able to observe from the outside; it was an extraordinary event as all these many streamed in on the central place in the theatre and became one thing, one being – a dragon made of light, that description will have to do, for what can I say about this?

The dragon made of light and a million souls loved us, it blessed us, and then it left us.

They went home.

It went home.

I already know that no matter how many nights are still to come, I will never be able to look up at the stars and not wonder if I don't see these dragons flying there, dancing, living and playing in realms of pure enchantment, leading their own lives, finding their own paths, going forward to their own unknowable unfoldments.

When it left, the theatre was left empty also, and there were only a few who had been left behind.

A few confused potentials stood amidst the swirling, sparkling ashes of their fellows who had gone, become a part of that the greatest of unfoldments known to us, and there were some of us here and there in the stands, and of course, there was me, and Margaret, Xiao Hong, Gaius, Mark, Adela, and Alexandra.

We were joined by the others who had been accorded the inordinate honour of becoming the seeds of the next unfoldment.

I already knew that Catherine was amongst them.

Nineteen of our kind, and nineteen potentials who would be our first Arada.

I was fascinated by oldest amongst us, one Meruvian.

He was far away, but never had I known such gladness, such joy; it was as though he was joy incarnate.

We all looked to him and fell silent. We bathed in his joy at the deliverance of those he loved; and in the knowledge that we would all meet again, in a different way, in a hundred thousand years from now, when there were once more enough of us to give birth to yet another being of light that would arise and live amongst the stars.

We would be there; we would have waited, whispering elders, in a special place of dream and gentle drifting, until the next time and we would be called, and we would too become a part of this unfoldment, this genesis, this evolution.

But until then, much work remained as yet undone.

It was up to us now to shape the next one hundred thousand years.

It was up to us to create a progression and society that would allow the souls to grow in safety, in gentle, precious care, slowly nurturing each other's paths, weaving a tapestry of souls and destinies that would eventually become so dense that it would breach the threshold – and once again, the one would come, and takes us home.

It was extraordinary.

It was exciting.

It was a blessing inordinate that I should be right here, and have become a part of this, and that I am allowed to serve at such a precious time, indeed.

Awe and wonderment fills me entirely.

The new unfoldment has begun.

- THE END -

ADDENDUM

Terms & Phrases

Assay -   *Title of a human servant assigned to a house. The Assay is the human representative of the house and in control of all material matters pertaining to the house.*

House - *A family of young vampires under one Docem.*

Underworld - *The place, usually underground, where the Arada dream.*

Festival Of Blessings - *Annual Winter Solstice gathering of vampires to choose the new generation of Arada and bind the community.*

Wilderness - *Territory outside of the Lower Covenant.*

Ascendance - *Evolving from one vampire level to the next.*

Potential - *A human who is allowed to attend the Festival Of Blessings and who may potentially become a vampire.*

Union - *Taking and giving life force.*

Riversmooth - *A state of being that shields the vampire inside from outside influences and allows them to remain calm and clear. Taught to young Cestra as a "child's exercise".*

Covenant - *The holy laws of the vampires, three in all: 1: Love, 2: Unfoldment, 3: Preciousness.*

Lower Covenant - *Rules pertaining to practical conduct in the vampire society*

Conversion - *An intervention or blessing that allows humans to see more than is ordinarily possible so they can interact with vampires. All potentials undergo conversions so they are able to partake in the dance of choosing at the Festival. It is an "enlightenment gift" the human retains, whether they are chosen or not.*

Transformation - *The process of becoming a vampire; the physical body dies but the energy system remains intact, and transformed into the vampire state.*

Numbers

1 - Arada

2 - Cestra

3 - Docem

4 - Ferata

5 - Segar

6 - Cardor

7 - Essem

8 - Taray

9 - Sedem

10 - Selest

11 - Sheza

12 - Ateen

13 - Ashla

14 - Denestra

15 - Catreen

16 - Epura

17 - Dardra

18 - Denest

19 - Cerren

Personae Dramatis

Valia

Meruvian

Mark Anthony Edwards

Steve Burrows

Adela Bach

Satari Elsherif

Alexandra Zyskowska

Gaius Decius Levinius

Xiao Hong

John Eldrich 3rd

Margaret Crawley

Vampire Ascendancy Levels

Arada

The Dreaming One: People in the process of turning into vampires as their energy system is being replaced and changed.

Cestra

The Walker Between Worlds: Newborn vampires who are cared for and educated in a house. Amongst their duties is to care for the Arada, and to discover, prepare and then bring new potentials to the Festival of Blessings.

Docem

The Master: Once a Cestra has engaged in a transformative First Union with a human, they become Docem, and responsible for the running of a house and all who live under their protection.

Ferata

The Wild One: When the Docem stage is completed, vampires will leave their house and live wild, sometimes for centuries, without any contact with other vampires, feeding on nature energies alone. A great deal of time is spent in unconscious rapport with creatures and nature occurrences. Ferata are the only vampire rank who does not ordinarily attend the Festival.

Segar

The One Who Walks Alone: After the Ferata stage, consciousness returns and the vampire will walk the Earth, observing, intervening, playing with all the Earth has to offer.

Cardor

The Keeper Of The Covenant: Once the Segar stage is being completed, the vampire knows enough to withdraw and study the mysteries of the Covenant, as well as adjusting the lower Covenant in light of the information retrieved in the preceding stages.

Essem

The Radiant One: The oldest present vampires. Little is known of their tasks and purposes, but they usually have concerns of their own and these are mysterious.

Taray

The Whispering Elder: When a vampire becomes too old, they lose cohesion and seem to disintegrate and "leave the planes" altogether. This causes intense bereavement in their chosen ones and their lines; so much so, that entire lines can go insane and tear themselves apart in shock and pain. This is held to be an evolutionary device to ensure cohesion and strength in those who survive.

Cestra Ta Docem

A Cestra rank Vampire who is ready to take on a conversion for the first time in order to transit into Docem. Out of all the ranks, this is the only one where someone acts outside the rank they are holding, and at the Festival of Blessings, is allowed to be on a level above their actual rank.